W9-DEU-530

Dark River Legacy

Also by B. J. Hoff
in Large Print:

The Captive Voice
The Penny Whistle
Storm at Daybreak
The Tangled Web

This Large Print Book carries the
Seal of Approval of N.A.V.H.

Dark River Legacy

B. J. HOFF

Thorndike Press • Thorndike, Maine

Published in 1999 by arrangement with Tyndale House Publishers, Inc.

Thorndike Large Print® Christian Mystery Series.

The tree indicium is a trademark of Thorndike Press.

The text of this Large Print edition is unabridged.
Other aspects of the book may vary from the original edition.

Set in 16 pt. Plantin.

Printed in the United States on permanent paper.

Library of Congress Cataloging in Publication Data

Hoff, B. J., 1940–
   Dark river legacy / B. J. Hoff.
      p.   cm. (Daybreak Mysteries, Book 5)
     ISBN 0-7862-1677-8 (lg. print : hc : alk. paper)
     1. Large type books.   I. Title.
   [PS3558.O34395D37 1999]
    813′.54—dc21   98-42032

When yesterday's bright dreams
dissolve to dust
and quickly scatter,
the Lord of Love comes near
to offer better things . . .
When everything in which
we've placed our trust
begins to crumble,
there's One who never fails —
the King of Kings . . .

B. J. Hoff
from *Banners of His Love*

PROLOGUE

Derry Ridge, Kentucky
Last week of May

An immense column of a man moved
steadily, almost woodenly, up the hillside.
His black clothing rendered him nearly invisible in the darkness. Even his white hair
was concealed, except for the burred sides,
by a black shooter's cap. His thick-pillared
legs carried him rapidly, spanning several
feet with each pace. On a sling he carried an
AK-47 rifle, and a 9mm Beretta with a silencer on a belt slide. Concealed in an ankle
rig was a .38 Bulldog. A pair of Israeli-
designed infrared goggles dangled from a
neck strap, tapping his massive chest as he
climbed.

The small white cabin just up the hill
was dark except for a dim glow, which he
assumed to be a night-light, seeping from a
rear window. It came on every night a little
after eleven, a moment after all the other
inside lights went dark. At the same time,
the outside security light mounted on a

pole to the left of the cabin would go on, beaming a pinkish gold spray across part of the side and most of the front yard.

He had been watching the cabin for four nights, and the routine hadn't varied more than a few minutes one way or the other.

The old lady might be crazy, but she was predictable.

It was a sultry night, sticky with late-spring humidity and sweet with the scent of wildflowers. He slapped automatically at a prickle on his heavily muscled upper arm; the bugs had been after him since sunset, and he wished he had worn a long-sleeved shirt, regardless of the heat.

The man climbed a few more feet, then stopped. With one hand on the stock of the rifle and the other splayed at his waist, he stood watching.

The cabin had the look of a little girl's playhouse. A neat flag-stone walk traced the path to the front steps. Frilly curtains trimmed the small, square windows, and a calico wreath hung on the door. The front edge of the porch was lined with a variety of flowering potted plants.

His mind replayed his orders: *Isolate her; question her; terminate her.* If she appeared to be even halfway rational — if there was a chance, no matter how slight, that she might have spilled anything about the *Lady A* — he was also to eliminate her entire circle of acquaintances. They couldn't afford the risk that the old ditz might have talked or, if she hadn't yet remembered, might do so at some point in the future.

From what he had seen so far, she wasn't tight with anyone except the teacher who lived down the hill, and he'd be easy enough to settle. He seemed to spend most of his time roaming the woods or talking with the college kids along the riverbank.

Just to be safe, he would watch another two or three days before making his move. Not so much to nail down her routine — he knew it pretty well by now — but to make certain there was no one else in her life, someone he might have missed. Someone she might have talked to.

In the meantime, he would take care of the security light, to make things easier when he was ready. Removing the silenced Beretta from his belt, the man aimed, fired once, and waited. The light popped with the first shot, and after a couple of seconds, he replaced the automatic in the slide and started back down the hill.

Without a backward glance, he retraced the route he had followed on the way up, veering right after a few yards to start around the ridge. He continued to walk until he reached an abandoned storage shed and a black van, both nearly obscured by a dense cover of trees.

Abby woke up slowly, blinking as her eyes attempted to focus. The room was quiet except for Peaches' soft purring at the foot of the bed and the rhythmic ticking of the alarm clock on the night table. She had left the window air conditioner turned on, but it wasn't running.

For several minutes she lay unmoving. The darkness of the bedroom was relieved only by the faint glow of a night-light plugged into the wall outlet. Beyond the open doorway, the hall was dark.

She pushed herself up on one arm, grimacing at the dull ache in her lower back as she moved. Reaching for her glasses with fingers stiff from sleep and arthritis, she put them on and squinted at the clock's luminescent hands.

Almost midnight.

What had awakened her? It wasn't unusual for her to wake up several times during the night, of course. She had never been a sound sleeper. At least she didn't think she had been. She couldn't remember the Time-before-the-Hospital, but since she'd come to the mountain, she was often restless at night.

Sometimes she dreamed — dark, cavernous dreams that wound through endless tunnels and shadowed chambers. Often she awoke frightened and bewildered, her heart pounding with an urgency to remember . . . something.

But the dreams would fade after she had been awake for a while, and along with them any trace of vague uneasiness.

She sighed, and the small cat sleeping at her feet stirred and yawned but didn't get up.

After another moment, she lifted a hand to remove her glasses, then stopped. A cold finger of apprehension touched the nape of her neck.

Something was wrong.

The faint golden rays from the security light usually filtered through the curtains, but now there was only a thick, inky darkness.

Flipping back the sheet, she pushed herself up, sitting on the side of the bed until the pain in her back ebbed. Then she got up and went to the window, lifted one corner of the ruffled yellow curtain, and peered outside.

Nothing. She pulled the curtain back a

little more but could still see only thick, obscure shadows. The security light was out.

It had been on when she went to bed, she was almost certain.

At a soft, questioning meow from Peaches, Abby turned back toward the bed. The small, orange-spotted cat stood up, stretched, then stared at her owner.

"Our outside light is burned out, Peaches," she said to the cat. "I suppose that doesn't bother you at all, though. You could see just fine out there, with or without the light, couldn't you? But I don't believe I care for it very much. Tomorrow we'll ask Mitch if he'll replace it for us. I'm sure he will, he —"

Abby jumped when the air conditioner suddenly switched on and churned to life, then shook her head at her own foolishness.

"My, I'm as nervous as a cat — excuse me, Peaches — jumping at every noise. There's nothing to be afraid of up here, is there, no matter how dark it is?"

She glanced out the window once more, then laid her glasses on the night table and went back to bed.

At her feet, Peaches padded around in a circle a couple of times before settling back into the nest she'd made earlier. After washing her face with her front paws, she curled up in a ball and closed her eyes.

ONE

Jennifer thought Derry Ridge, Kentucky, must be about as far removed from life in the fast lane as an Amish farm would be from Times Square. It was a setting that invited contentment, a place that enticed you to relax a little and dream a lot.

The hillside across the river from the campus was a deep, lush green, the May woods spotted with pink dogwoods and yellow forsythia. The air was spiced with the rich smells of things blooming and growing in fertile soil. Even the sounds around her hinted of new beginnings and fresh hope. Birds sang and honeybees buzzed, and in the background was the ever present harmony of the Derry River, running clean and strong and constant.

Jennifer yawned and turned to look at her drowsy husband. Daniel's eyes were closed, his chin lifted toward the early afternoon sun. A soft golden haze and flickering shadows dappled the strong lines of his face. Sunny, his guide dog, lay peacefully at her master's feet, her paws nestled snugly under her chin. Jennifer smiled.

"It's incredibly beautiful here, Daniel."

"Mm-hm."

"I wish you could see it, especially the colors. They're —" Jennifer searched for a description he could visualize clearly. "Easter egg colors."

One eyebrow quirked a little. "Mm."

Half-asleep, just as she'd suspected. "I think this must be what the British Isles look like in the spring. No wonder Mitch goes on so about his home state."

Daniel nodded.

"You know, he isn't quite what I expected."

Daniel slouched against the picnic bench, stretching his long legs even farther out in front of him. "How's that?" It was a halfhearted question.

"Oh, I don't know. I think I was expecting him to be more —" Jennifer stopped to think. "More *intellectual*. You know, bookish. Maybe a little forgetful."

With obvious reluctance, Daniel sat up, ran a hand over the back of his neck, then slipped his arm around her shoulder. "The absentminded professor stereotype?"

"Yes, I suppose so. He's certainly proved me wrong."

Again Jennifer scanned their surroundings. Across the grounds to her right, the

15

chapel clock struck two, but the sound was muffled by a large group of boisterous young people making their way from the student center to the parking lot.

"He seems awfully *tense*, don't you think?" she said, her thoughts returning to Mitch Donovan.

"Maybe a little." Daniel paused. "He did walk the floor most of last night."

Jennifer turned to look at him. "If you heard him walking the floor, then you must not have slept well either."

He shrugged, brushing a fly away from his arm. "I never get much sleep the first night away from home."

Abruptly, Jennifer sat up. "You don't suppose there's something wrong, do you? Maybe we should have stayed at the Lodge after all."

Daniel shook his head. "Mitch wouldn't have it. Ever since we agreed to do the workshop, he's insisted that we stay with him. I imagine he's just keyed up about this festival. Coordinating the whole thing has to be a lot of work."

"I hope that's all it is." Jennifer rested her head on Daniel's shoulder. "He seems awfully nice. And kind. I think he's a very kind man." She glanced up at him. "I wonder why he's not married yet."

16

Daniel shook his head, grinning. "You have a real problem with the idea of a man over thirty who's still single, don't you, darlin'?"

"Most men are married by the time they're thirty, Daniel," she reminded him archly.

"I wasn't."

"That's different. You were waiting for me."

"Smartest decision I ever made, too," he said agreeably.

"Mm. Well, maybe he's engaged," she said, distracted by her study of Daniel's profile.

"Mitch? I don't think so. He's never mentioned anyone special, and the way I go on about you, I imagine he'd say something if he had a lady in his life."

Jennifer smiled to herself, pleased at the thought of her husband "going on about her." "Odd. He's so nice, I would have thought —"

She stopped when she saw the subject of their conversation walking across the lawn toward them. "Here he comes now."

Mitch Donovan crossed the grounds with an easy, ambling stride. Still, Jennifer sensed the same undercurrent of tension hovering about him that she had felt at their first meeting the day before.

A tall, rangy man in his early thirties, he approached with his head down, his shoulders hunched slightly forward as if burdened by an invisible weight. His curly, dark copper hair had trapped a spray of sunshine and appeared to be shot with gold dust — a fiery, glistening contrast to his much darker beard.

Daniel had met the professor from Kentucky at a youth rally in Clarksburg, West Virginia, two years earlier. Their mutual interest in music, particularly Appalachian folk and contemporary Christian, had launched a long-distance friendship.

As the director of the Kentucky Heritage Department, Mitch coordinated an annual Heritage Arts Festival. Each year the week-long event focused on a different kind of music, offering workshops and concerts by various artists. This year, contemporary Christian music was to be featured, and Mitch had invited the Kaines to lead one of the workshops.

The likelihood that her own invitation was merely a courtesy didn't bother Jennifer in the least. She simply applauded Mitch's good sense for recognizing the contribution Daniel would make to the festival. A gifted composer in his own right,

Daniel had begun to gain widespread attention. *Daybreak*, a musical drama he had written after being blinded, had met with astonishing success; its title song was still frequently recorded by artists in the contemporary Christian music industry. More recently, the popular husband-and-wife team of Paul Alexander and Vali Tremayne had recorded a number of Daniel's songs on their albums, all of which shot to the top of the charts as soon as they were released.

Now that they were here, Jennifer was more enthusiastic than ever about the week ahead. The workshops should be fun, and she was excited about the prospect of meeting some of the celebrities who would be in attendance. Lifestream, one of the most popular singing groups in Christian music — and a favorite of Daniel's — was to give a concert on Friday.

But she was far more excited about another guest, one who had nothing to do with music. The brochure Mitch had mailed them had featured an announcement that the internationally acclaimed novelist, Gwynevere Leigh — America's First Lady of Mystery — would be returning to her hometown to lead a creative writing workshop during the festival.

Jennifer was determined to meet the young author who had stunned the publishing world with two best-selling novels before she graduated from college. She had packed her brand-new copy of Leigh's most recent book with the hope of having it autographed.

All things considered, the week promised to be one to remember.

"All things considered," Mitch announced without preamble as he came to stand in front of them, "this week promises to be a real challenge." His tone was grim, his expression strained.

"Something wrong?" Daniel asked.

Mitch glanced back over his shoulder at the river, at the same time jingling a ring of keys in one hand.

"I was counting on having all the concerts and most of the workshops outdoors," he explained, turning back to them. "Our auditorium is too small for the concerts, and last year some of the workshops were standing room only, too. But I just heard the weather forecast for the week."

"Bad?" Daniel stretched, then got to his feet.

"Miserable. Rain most of the week. *Heavy* rain. Starting tomorrow."

Daniel slipped his hands into his pockets. "Maybe it'll change directions."

"Let's hope."

"We'll help any way we can," Jennifer offered. "Just let us know what we can do." She hesitated, uncertain as to whether this was the right time, yet too eager to wait. "Mitch, could I ask *you* a favor for sometime this week?"

Mitch pocketed the keys. "I'll surely try," he said, smiling. "What do you need?"

"Well . . . I'm a big fan of Gwynevere Leigh," Jennifer explained. "I was wondering if you could arrange for me to meet her, at least long enough to get her autograph. I couldn't believe it when I saw that she's going to be here this week — and that she used to *live* here! Did you know her?"

As Jennifer watched, his smile faded. The lean angles of his face seemed to sharpen even more, and the glint of amusement disappeared from his eyes.

He delayed his answer just long enough to make Jennifer wonder if she shouldn't have asked. Finally, his expression cleared. "I . . . used to know her, yes. Well enough to get you an autograph, anyway."

"Wonderful!"

Avoiding her gaze, Mitch changed the subject. "We'd better get the two of you acquainted with the campus while the weather's still good. Feel like taking a walk?" Without waiting for a reply, he put a hand on Daniel's shoulder. "Why don't we start with Johnson Hall? That's where your workshop will be if it rains."

During the next hour, Mitch took them on a tour of the campus. He was an enthusiastic guide; his love for the college and the town of Derry Ridge was unmistakable. Jennifer noted that his relationship with other faculty members and students seemed to be one of mutual respect and liking. A quick, natural friendliness was apparent between Mitch and everyone they met as they crossed the campus.

"Let's head toward the cafeteria," he suggested as they left the language arts building. "I could do with a cup of coffee."

"I'm surprised at how many students are on campus this time of year," Jennifer said, stopping at the edge of a curb. "The semester's over, isn't it?"

Mitch nodded, then quickly replied, "It is, but most of the students either stay on campus or come back for the festival. It's become a kind of tradition." He watched as Sunny led Daniel around a loose chunk of concrete. "Take a right after we get across the parking lot, Dan. Does Sunny handle crowds all right, by the way? It's likely to be pretty crazy by tomorrow."

"She'll be fine," Daniel replied, stepping up onto the sidewalk and turning right, as Mitch had directed. "Seeing Eye dogs get plenty of training in crowd control before they graduate. Sunny's a people dog."

"She's a beauty, too," Mitch observed, smiling at the retriever.

"She makes a big difference in my life," Daniel acknowledged. He paused a beat, then grinned. "Just like my other lady."

"Nice of you to include me," Jennifer said dryly.

Unexpectedly, Mitch stopped. "Well now, here comes the special lady in *my* life," he said, smiling and lifting a hand in greeting.

Pleased by the revelation that there was a woman in Mitch's life after all, Jennifer turned to look. It took her a moment to realize that the subject of Mitch's attention was the diminutive, round-faced woman who was hurrying toward them.

"Mitch! Oh, I'm so glad I finally found you!" The small, plump woman, who looked to be in her early sixties, was clearly agitated. Her words tumbled out in a rush as she stood clenching and unclenching her hands at her waist.

"They told me you were in the chapel, but you weren't." She tilted her head in order to look up at Mitch.

He stooped slightly, smiling down at her. "What's the matter, Abby? Peaches didn't run off again, did she?"

"Peaches?" The woman looked at him. "Oh, no. No, Peaches is at home, Mitch. I was afraid to let her out this morning."

Mitch frowned. "Why would you be afraid to let Peaches out?"

"Because of what happened last night. I was afraid she might get hurt."

Mitch's frown deepened. "Last night? What happened last night?"

Abby visibly relaxed the moment Mitch took her hand.

"That's what I'm trying to tell you. That's why I didn't come to church this morning. Did you look for me?"

"I did, yes, but by the time I went downstairs with the choir and got out of my robe, I figured you'd already left. Now, what's this about last night? What happened?"

"I don't like it, Mitch! I don't like it at all. It was probably one of those vandals you told me about, playing a trick on me, but it made me nervous."

Mitch's gaze roamed over the woman's

tousled, gray-blonde hair, then scanned the circle of her face. A pretty face, Jennifer noted, wide-eyed and sweet despite the inexpertly applied makeup. It was the kind of face you would instinctively trust, she thought, with features reminiscent of a favorite grandmother or aunt. Again, she wondered about Abby's place in Mitch Donovan's life.

"Abby, tell me what happened." Mitch's voice was kind, his affection for the woman impossible to miss.

"The security light outside the cabin, Mitch — it's completely shattered. I think somebody shot it out."

"Shot it out?" Mitch's good-natured expression turned hard. "When?"

"Last night," Abby said with obvious impatience. "Didn't I just tell you that, dear? Will you fix it for me?"

After a couple of seconds, he nodded distractedly. "Sure, I'll fix it," he answered, still holding her hand. "Abby, do you have any idea what time that might have been? Did you see anyone?"

Calmer now, Abby shook her head. "No, I woke up a little before midnight, and when I looked out there wasn't a bit of light. The only thing I found this morning was a lot of glass around the bottom of the pole."

She paused, darting an almost apologetic glance toward Jennifer and Daniel before going on in a quieter tone of voice. "It's awfully dark outside without the light, Mitch. Do you think you could fix it soon?"

Mitch hesitated. "I don't think I can do it before tomorrow, Abby."

Her face crumpled.

"It's Sunday, sweetheart," Mitch reminded her gently. "I doubt that I can find a replacement today." He paused. "Tell you what, I have a floodlight we can hook up this evening, until I can fix the pole lamp. That should do almost as well. All right?"

Abby's relief was evident. "I knew you'd think of something, Mitch," she said, reaching up to pat his bearded face with a chubby hand. "You always do."

Mitch grinned down at her. "Come over here; I want you to meet some friends. Remember, I told you about Daniel and Jennifer, that they'd be staying with me this week?"

Abby already seemed to know a great deal about the Kaines. "But where's your little boy?" she asked abruptly after the introductions had been made. "Didn't he come too?"

Abby's face fell when Jennifer explained that Jason was staying with Daniel's family for the week. "Oh, dear, and I made *cookies* for him. Chocolate chip and peanut butter and pineapple crunch and . . . oh, well . . ."

Moving in a little closer, Daniel flashed a smile in Abby's direction. "In Jason's absence, Abby, I'd be happy to take those cookies off your hands."

She beamed up at him. "Well now, you can have just as many as you want, Daniel. I've made hundreds this week, for the fellowship time after the concerts. And for Mitch, too, of course."

Pausing only for a split second, Abby turned to Jennifer. "Aren't you terribly proud of your husband, dear? I have a tape of *Daybreak* and a Vali Tremayne tape with some of Daniel's songs on it. He writes such beautiful music, doesn't he? I listen to music all the time, and I simply love Daniel's."

She caught another quick breath before rushing on. "Mitch promised to bring you to visit this week. My cabin is just up the hill from his. Mitch and some of the young people fixed it up for me, painted it inside and out — it's just like new. He's wonderfully handy," she added in a soft, conspiratorial tone, "for a musician."

Jennifer pressed Daniel's arm and saw him grin in response. Mitch's Abby was an absolute delight.

"Well, dear," the woman said, turning back to Mitch, "I have to run. Mrs. Snider is waiting for me in the cafeteria."

"You're working this afternoon?" Mitch asked. "You weren't in there at lunchtime, were you?"

"No, no, I just came down to help get the macaroni salad and baked beans ready for tomorrow, so we don't have to do it later. I want to hear your choir tonight."

Mitch reassured her one more time that he would take care of an outside light for her by evening, and Abby bustled off, all signs of her earlier anxiety gone.

"She's *wonderful!*" Jennifer told him, watching Abby bounce down the concrete walk. "Are the two of you related?"

Still smiling, Mitch shook his head. "No, no relation. We just kind of — adopted each other. As a matter of fact, nobody really knows who Abby is. Or where she came from."

Curious, Jennifer kept her hand on Daniel's arm as they started to walk toward the sprawling brick student center. "She's not from here then?"

"No," Mitch replied. "Abby started

showing up on campus every day several months ago. She'd walk around the grounds and talk to the students. Sometimes she'd slip into the back of the chapel for worship but then leave as soon as it was over. One of the counselors found out she was living like a bag lady in an equipment shed up on the hill behind the girls' dorms. Eventually, the senior class and some of the faculty took her under their wings and fixed up an abandoned cabin for her, just up the ridge from my place. She's been living there ever since."

"You have no idea where she's from?" asked Daniel.

Mitch shook his head. "Not a clue. We don't even know her last name. *She* doesn't know it."

The image of Abby's sweetly attractive face with its guileless smile nagged at Jennifer. What could possibly have forced a woman like that into such destitute circumstances?

"Amnesia?" Daniel asked, as if reading Jennifer's thoughts.

Mitch hesitated, then nodded. "So it would seem. Although she does remember a few things. She told us that she came here on a bus. She remembered being in a hospital, but she doesn't know where it was. She seems to recall things about a certain room, a room with light blue walls and a painting of a dove."

Daniel stopped walking, bringing Jennifer up short with him. "Did you try to trace her background?"

Mitch shrugged. "The local police supposedly made inquiries, but our police department isn't really equipped to do much more than direct traffic and round up Saturday night drunks."

"What about this business with her yard light?"

"We've had a lot of vandalism around town for the past year or so. Most of it from teenagers, I'm afraid. Our dropout rate is high all over the county — a lot of kids are getting into trouble just because they don't have anything else to do. I'll call the police about it, but I doubt if they'll be much help."

"You said Abby remembered something about a hospital." Daniel's curiosity was obviously piqued. "Had Abby been ill, do you think?"

"She seemed perfectly all right to me," Mitch replied. "Oh, some of the people in town think she's a little odd, but she's not, really. She's . . . flighty, maybe, and she forgets things. But the administration gave her a job in the cafeteria, and she was practically running the place within two weeks. She can actually be very efficient. It seems to me that the only thing wrong with Abby is that she's obviously had some rough breaks in her life."

Jennifer studied Mitch's profile as he and Daniel talked. He had a good face, she decided. A kind and sensitive, gentle face. She felt instinctively that Mitch Donovan was a good man.

But not an altogether happy man. In spite of the laugh lines that creased the corners of those deep-set, golden brown eyes, his gaze was vulnerable — and not entirely trusting.

"The one thing we *do* know for certain about Abby," Mitch was saying, "is that she's a Christian. She had a small Bible with her, and she's well acquainted with its contents." A soft smile crossed his face. "She may not know where she came from, but she knows exactly where she's going. One of the Bible professors here has a saying that I think relates extremely well to Abby: 'You have to get to the point where Jesus Christ is all you *have* before you realize that Jesus Christ is all you *need.*' "

Still smiling, he added quietly, "As far as Abby's concerned, she's got everything she needs. And a lot more than money can buy."

"Speaking of what money can buy —," Jennifer interrupted, her attention caught by a sleek, silver Mercedes easing into a parking space on the opposite side of the lot. The door on the driver's side opened. Jennifer stared in unabashed admiration as a slender, raven-haired young woman stepped out of the car, straightened, and took a long, thorough look at her surroundings.

Jennifer heard Mitch catch a sharp breath. She turned and saw that his face was ashen, his hands trembling. He looked, she thought, like a man who had just witnessed a major disaster.

Again Jennifer's gaze went to the driver of the Mercedes. She was tall, taller than Jennifer's five-eight, and willow slim in a flamboyant peasant dress that would have been outrageous on anyone else. Long, glossy black hair emphasized the pale oval of a face that, even from this distance, was a striking display of high cheekbones and enormous eyes.

It took Jennifer another moment to realize why the face was so familiar. "That's *her.*"

Daniel lifted one dark, questioning brow. "Who?"

Instead of answering, Jennifer turned excitedly to Mitch. "That *is* Gwynevere Leigh, isn't it? I've seen her picture on book jackets."

The generous curve of Mitch's mouth had tightened into a hard line. A peculiar, almost feverish glint burned behind his eyes, and he took a sudden step backward as if he were about to turn and run. Finally, after what appeared to be an enormous struggle, he expelled a long breath and answered Jennifer. "Yes, that's her."

At that moment the woman turned toward them. She stood unmoving for a long time, her eyes locked on Mitch. At last she began to walk, slowly at first, then a little faster, her gaze never leaving Mitch's face as she approached.

Jennifer thought she could almost hear the crackle of electricity arcing between Mitch Donovan and the striking young author as she approached.

She stopped directly in front of Mitch, lifting her chin in a gesture that seemed oddly defiant — and in direct contrast to her uncertain smile. She stood studying him in silence.

Her voice was surprisingly soft when she finally spoke. "Hello, Mitch." She seemed to hold her breath once the words were out.

Jennifer looked at Mitch. He appeared to be having difficulty swallowing but otherwise seemed to have regained control. The only sign of his earlier discomfiture was the faint glaze of pain in his eyes.

"Hello, Freddi," he said quietly after an awkward silence. "Welcome home."

Jennifer saw the look that passed between them and pressed Daniel's arm to indicate that an exit was in order. "Let's get some coffee, Daniel," she said.

It was obvious that no one except her husband heard a word she said.

TWO

He had rehearsed this scene in his mind a hundred times or more since learning that she was coming back, but not once had he come close to anticipating the brutal, dizzying pain that now ripped through him.

For a moment Mitch felt a desperate, childish desire to turn and run. He thought he was going to make a total fool of himself. Instead, he could only stand gawking at her, drinking in the sight of her, frantically battling to still the wild storm raging inside his head.

It was as if he were eighteen all over again — eighteen and hopelessly, helplessly, foolishly in love.

The years, it seemed, hadn't really passed at all. It had been only a dream, a cruel, mocking dream, those dismal years without her. Time couldn't have passed. It must have merely hung suspended. Nothing had changed. She hadn't changed . . . not all that much. She was thinner. Too thin. But she still had style.

She had always had style. Even in a baseball cap and sweatshirt, she had exuded a kind of elegant unconventionality, a distinctive flair that made her . . . Freddi.

Strange, how naturally the affectionate nickname he had given her in junior high had spilled from his lips. It occurred to him that this more mature, sophisticated Gwynevere Leigh might resent being called *Freddi.*

And yet it still seemed to fit her.

"You're looking good, Mitch."

She was looking like yesterday. The long sweep of midnight-silk hair still framed a fair, fresh complexion. The nose still turned up a little too much to be perfect, and the deep gray eyes were still unnervingly steady and measuring. As he remembered, she wore no makeup; the faint blush touching her cheeks and lips was natural.

Her grandfather had sometimes fondly called her "Snow White," and Mitch, finding the comparison intriguingly appropriate, had occasionally echoed it.

"Then that makes you my prince," she would reply archly.

A pain knifed through him, the kind of pain he hadn't felt since those long, punishing months after she left. He felt himself sway slightly and hoped she hadn't noticed.

Dimly aware that he needed to say something, Mitch swallowed against the dryness of his throat. "How have you been?" he ventured thickly.

Now that's an opener with real punch, Donovan. Maybe you should have been a writer, too. . . .

The familiar grin appeared — that impish, gently taunting grin with its hint of challenge, its faint tilt of mischief. Was it a shade less confident now, or was he only imagining the unfamiliar softness around her mouth?

She surprised him by giving an uncertain little shrug. "I'm fine. At least I will be after my stomach stops heaving."

Mitch frowned.

Freddi glanced over her shoulder toward the parking lot and the highway beyond. "Some creep in a black van ran me off the road. I just about went over the drop at the dam trying to get out of his way."

Mitch was finding it difficult to take in her words. His head pounded with the sight of her; his mind seemed frozen. "Are you all right?" His voice sounded harsh, even to himself.

Freddi tossed off his question with an indifferent wave of her hand. "Just aggravated." She looked at him. "So, Mitch — I suppose I should call you 'professor' now."

"Associate professor," he corrected.

Even her voice was the same. Soft but direct, poised but with a note of amusement lurking just below the surface, as if at any moment she might break into that full-throated laugh of hers that always made everyone else laugh with her.

He hadn't believed she would come, had even made a hasty attempt to dissuade the language arts committee from inviting her. When he heard that she had accepted, he had still been certain she would back out at the last minute. *If only she had . . .*

He looked at her to find her studying his face with an intensity that made his throat tighten and close.

"This is what you always wanted. I'm glad for you, Mitch."

What I always wanted was you, Freddi . . . more than anything else . . . and you knew it.

He tried to force a smile. "This is a surprise," he managed, "seeing you here."

"You didn't know I was coming?"

"I knew," he said too quickly. "I just wasn't sure —"

"That I'd show up?" she finished for him, her wide, high brows lifting speculatively.

He shrugged his answer. "Will you be here . . . all week?" He made himself meet her eyes, again felt his control start to slip away.

She looked back at him, unhurriedly studying his face before answering. "Actually, I'm thinking about staying."

Something flared deep inside Mitch, a small spark of hope, quickly doused by a wave of panic. "Staying?"

Freddi nodded. "There's a potential buyer for the farm. I don't think I want to sell, but the estate can't be settled until I decide. I thought I should stay around for a while before making any decisions."

Mitch fought against his rioting emotions. How much longer was he going to be able to stand here, dizzy with the heady scent of her cologne, melting under those enormous, searching eyes?

"I, ah, I'm sorry I wasn't here," he stammered, "when your grandfather died." It had been nine years since he had seen her. She had been in town two years ago for her grandfather's funeral, but he had been on vacation. Relief had mingled with disappointment when he returned and heard that he had missed her.

"You were in Canada."

He shot her a surprised look.

"I asked around. I had hoped to see you."

Mitch changed the subject. "It's taken all this time to find a buyer for the farm?" *How long could they volley this meaningless small talk back and forth without really saying anything?*

Freddi shrugged. "It's a lot of land, a big risk with the way things are for farmers these days."

Mitch nodded in agreement, shifting from one foot to the other. "I should be going," he said abruptly, starting to move away even as he spoke. "I promised to show Dan and Jennifer around the campus. They're probably waiting for me." He hesitated. "It's — been great seeing you again, Freddi."

"Mitch." Her voice was low but insistent.

He froze, dragging his gaze to her face.

"You're —" She glanced at his left hand, then met his eyes. "Are you married?"

Resentment welled up in him. He felt himself flush as he stared at her. "No."

"Neither am I," she said softly.

"I know," Mitch blurted out before he thought. In spite of his resolve to forget her, he read her press regularly. There had been a man once, a brief engagement that apparently hadn't worked.

His eyes locked with hers and clung. After an awkward silence, Freddi glanced away. "I thought . . . maybe we could get together," she said quietly, "to catch up on one another."

Slowly she looked back to him, waiting.

Angry with his own lack of composure, he forced a note of brightness into his voice. "Sure. I want to hear all about your life. It may be hard to find the time this week, though. There's a lot going on. . . ." Feeling awkward and glaringly transparent, he let his voice trail off.

"What about after the musical tonight?"

His hands were trembling, and he shoved them into his pockets. "The musical? You're coming?"

"I thought I would." She smiled at him. "You're directing it, aren't you?"

He nodded stiffly as his mind sped forward, then lurched in reverse, scrambling for an excuse. "I — I'm not sure, Freddi. I have company for the week — the couple that was just here. They'll be going back to my place with me, after we rig up a floodlight up at Abby's —"

"Abby?"

Quickly he explained about Abby and the security light.

When she remained quiet, he looked away for an instant, then back to her. *Don't be a fool. . . . You don't have to do this. You don't owe her anything.*

"I suppose . . . you could join us." *You jerk . . . what, you're going to offer her homemade ice cream and cookies next? Maybe she'd like a piece of your heart, too. She took most of it with her nine years ago anyway; you might as well let her have the rest.*

She searched his eyes. "Really? I wouldn't be intruding?"

Oh, no, not a bit . . . no more than a knife through my heart. . . .

"No, not at all," he came back, trying his best to sound casual. "You could sit with the Kaines . . . and Abby . . . during the musical, if you like." At her quick nod of agreement, he hurried on. "We can all meet afterward and go to my place."

"I'd like that," she said without hesitating. "If your friends won't mind."

He tried to clear his throat, but managed only a choking sound. "I'm sure they won't."

"Good. Well, I suppose I should sign in, or whatever it is I'm supposed to do today. Could you show me where the registration office is?"

"You need to go to the lobby in the student center," Mitch said, eager to get away from that studying gaze. "That's where I was headed."

As always, she walked as if she knew exactly where she was going, giving her surroundings a sweeping appraisal along the way.

"Where are you staying?" Mitch asked as they started toward the entrance.

"I had planned to stay at the farm, but it will be another day or two before Mrs. Kraker gets the house aired out and the kitchen stocked for me. I'm at the Lodge for now." She smiled at him, and the ache began all over again.

The Lodge. He had worked there all the way through high school. Bits and pieces of memories began to unroll, whipping through his mind with lightning speed and clarity. . . .

The little-girl Freddi tugging at his hand just inside the park entrance to Briar Rose Glen, her thin face flushed with awe at the sight of a doe and its fawn poised in the twilight shadows . . . A twelve-year-old Freddi beside him on a scented summer morning, walking him to work on her way to a tennis lesson, her sunburned nose beginning to peel, her baseball cap tilted back over her ponytail . . . A teenage

Freddi, leaning contentedly against his shoulder as they watched the sun fold itself up and slip lazily down behind Vision Lake on a warm, sultry August evening . . . A grown-up Freddi pressing her face against his shoulder the night before she left for Ohio State . . .

"I have to try, Mitch. If I stay here, I'll never know whether I could have made it or not. At least understand why I have to try. I'll come back to you, Mitch; I promise you — I'll come back."

Nine years later, she was back.

Freddi watched him out of the corner of her eye as they approached the front doors of the center, still somewhat dazed by how different he was — and yet so much the same.

All those years ago, when he had been more than a boy yet not quite a man, she had sometimes caught a fleeting glimpse of what he promised to be . . . someday.

Now it was someday. And he was more, much more, than she had ever dreamed he would be.

The wiry, always too-thin boy with the sad, haunted eyes and the uncertain, vulnerable smile was no longer too thin, no longer a boy. Now he moved with the slender, confident grace of a man who knew himself — who he was, what he was doing, where he was going — and was comfortable with what he knew. The light spray of freckles across the bridge of his nose was nearly obscured by the bronze of his skin, and the deep cleft in his chin was hidden by a dark, closely trimmed beard. His hair, still thick and springy, was a little longer but not quite so curly as she remembered. And although he was still lean and lanky — she had often teased him that he looked like a hungry cowboy — his shoulders were now wider, his jaw stronger. He no longer looked hungry, though he still looked a little like a cowboy. Now, more than anything else, he looked like a man who had finally found what he wanted.

But those eyes . . . the eyes were still sad, and the smile was still vulnerable.

He was still Mitch. Mitch, who could stab her heart and shatter her defenses with one tender look, one soft word of affection, one gentle touch of caring.

Instinctively, Freddi tried to raise a protective wall, a barrier between her emotions and his profile. Then she remembered that she was done with walls.

"So — tell me about your friends," she

said, more in an attempt to get him to look at her again than to make conversation.

"Dan and Jennifer?" He kept his gaze straight ahead. "They're really special. I think you'll like them."

"Was that a guide dog with them?"

"Yes. Dan's blind." He paused. "A car accident. The other driver was drunk."

Freddi grimaced. "Is he one of the faculty?"

"No, they're just here for the festival. Dan's going to lead one of the workshops," Mitch explained. "He owns a Christian radio station in West Virginia. And he writes music — really *good* music."

His smile brightened a little, and he finally looked at her. "Do you remember the Olympics several years ago? You probably would have still been in junior high — about that time."

Freddi shrugged. "Not really. Why?"

"There was an American swimmer from West Virginia who won a gold. They called him the 'Swimming Machine.' "

Freddi thought for a minute. "I did some research on the Olympics for a book a few years ago. I remember something about that — the 'Swimming Machine' — I think."

"That was Dan," Mitch said, opening

one of the double doors to the student center and waiting for her to step through. "Daniel Kaine."

She stopped halfway through the door. "Really?" A memory flashed through her mind, an image of dark hair, a flushed face, eyes clouded with tears as a gold medal was slipped over his head.

"How does a man like that cope with being blind?" she mused, more to herself as they walked into the lobby.

"Extremely well, as a matter of fact," Mitch said.

There were only a few people inside the lobby, most of them scattered around the lounge area off to the right. Freddi glanced at Mitch and found him studying her. She thought he seemed slightly less awkward now. Still uncomfortable, but at least his eyes had lost that wild, desperate glint that made her feel as if he wanted nothing more than to bolt and run.

His gaze was openly questioning, as if he were looking for answers, probing her thoughts. It hurt to see the doubt, the un-certainty, in those eyes that had once looked at her with only warmth and affection.

"You'll need to go down there," he finally said, pointing to a table at the far end of the long, narrow hall. "The lady in the blue blouse should have everything you need."

Freddi glanced in the direction of his gesture, then turned back. "I'll see you later tonight, then?"

He seemed eager to get away. "Right. I'll look you up before the music starts. Come a little early if you can, so you can meet Dan and Jennifer — and Abby." He left her then, walking quickly, as if he could barely restrain himself from running.

Unable to look away from him until he turned the corner and disappeared, Freddi drew the first deep breath she had been able to catch since meeting him in the parking lot.

Her heart had soared at the sight of him, only to plummet at the bitterness and hurt she encountered when they faced one another. But at least he wasn't married, she reminded herself. She had been afraid he might be by now.

Married or not, the past is dead. . . . He's a man you haven't seen for years, not the boy who would have died for you. . . . That was yesterday . . . this is today.

Still, she had held on to enough of yesterday to give her hope. And it was that hope that had brought her home. Mitch was still Mitch, boy-become-man, but the same Mitch who had once known her better than anyone else . . . the Mitch who had grown up protecting her, defending her . . . loving her. . . .

Freddi glanced around the half-empty hallway. This was Mitch's place, his dream — the dream he had found in the very surroundings she had been so eager to leave.

Now she was back, searching for that long-ago dream of her own. During the darkest hour of one seemingly endless night, she had finally realized that her own dream had continued to elude her, to slip always just beyond her grasp, because she had left it here — right here in Derry Ridge.

Somewhere in this town, on this mountain, in the angry, accusing eyes of the man who had just left her, was whatever might remain of that dream. And no matter what the cost, she had to learn for herself whether she could reclaim what was left.

Freddi had made a number of new beginnings over the past few months. This one, she knew, was certain to be the most difficult of all.

THREE

The evening was deceptively tranquil, a contradiction to the maelstrom of Freddi's emotions.

Sweet and warm, the summerlike breeze was faintly scented with wildflowers and anticipation. The gentle, lulling sound of the nearby Derry River could be heard during the few seconds of silence preceding the musical's finale, and lanterns bathed the descending twilight with flickering gold.

Hundreds of people were gathered on the lawn. Some had brought their own chairs; others shared blankets on the ground. After coaxing both Daniel and Jennifer to sing with the choir, Mitch had set up chairs for Abby and Freddi near the wooden platform erected for the choir.

Freddi liked the Kaines and had immediately warmed to the vivacious, dark-eyed Jennifer with her unassuming friendliness and the tall, powerful-looking Daniel with his gentle smile and hearty laugh. She particularly appreciated the way both of them had displayed, after the first few awkward moments of introduction, more interest in her as a person than as a celebrity.

Once the performance had begun, Freddi found it unsettling, even disturbing, to watch Mitch. With consummate skill and sensitivity, he evoked from the singers a rich, triumphant offering of music that soared above the campus lawn and echoed out across the valley. Several times she had to fight back tears at the remembrance of things past . . . and things lost.

In the instant's hush before the final number, Freddi allowed her attention to wander for the first time in nearly an hour. Something off in the distance to her left caught her attention, and she straightened a little in the lawn chair to get a better look.

The man would have been impossible to miss. A huge, towering column in black, he stood on an incline that flanked the left side of the chapel, several yards away from the outside fringe of the crowd.

Sinister, Freddi thought as she studied him. He was immense, several inches over six feet, with the massive, heavily muscled frame of a professional bodybuilder. His skin was remarkably white, nearly as white as his hair, of which only a military-short burr was visible around the sides of a black shooter's cap.

She couldn't see his eyes. In spite of the fact that dusk was rapidly settling over the mountain, he wore a pair of dark aviator glasses. An involuntary shiver snaked along the back of Freddi's neck as she wondered about the eyes behind the glasses. She had the unnerving sensation that they might be carefully and deliberately scrutinizing every face in the crowd and committing each to memory.

Freddi had spent too many years gathering research in police stations and courtrooms not to react to such a blatantly suspicious-looking figure. Her eyes narrowed in speculation as she continued to study his hulking frame. Instinct told her that he was most likely carrying a gun, although none was visible.

Carefully, she unzipped the side pouch of her handbag and withdrew a slimline camera no larger than a compact. Palming it, she lifted her hand to her face as if to glance in a mirror, then smoothly released the shutter. Dropping the camera back into her purse, she returned her attention to the choir, whose voices were now climbing toward the majestic climax of the musical.

During the almost deafening ovation that greeted the finale, Freddi glanced once more toward the gentle swell of ground beside the chapel. The man was gone, but a lingering uneasiness chilled her as she stared into the thickening shadows that were beginning to cloak the campus.

The atmosphere in Mitch's living room later that night was, at best, tense. With a pang of sympathy for him, Jennifer noted the tightness around his eyes, the slight trembling of his hands every time his gaze encountered Freddi's.

He seemed to be trying a little too hard to be carefully polite to Freddi. Her response appeared to be a combination of restrained emotion and something very much like disappointment.

The problem seemed to be that neither Freddi nor Mitch could keep their eyes off one another for more than a moment or two. Every look that passed between them was charged with tension. Every word exchanged seemed laced with hidden meaning. There had been laughter and good-natured teasing while they were setting up the floodlight at Abby's cabin, but now a blanket of constraint had fallen over the room. The laughter seemed forced, the conversation stiff.

It was Abby who had unknowingly honed the tension of the evening to its peak. By ten o'clock they had consumed nearly two dozen cookies and a pot of coffee. Jennifer was sitting next to Daniel on the enormous sofa that rimmed one entire wall of the living room, while Mitch stood in front of the wide, stone fireplace facing them. Freddi had settled herself into a massive leather easy chair, her feet tucked snugly beneath her. She looked comfortably — though deceptively, Jennifer suspected — at ease with her surroundings.

Abby was on her way back from the kitchen with a fresh pot of coffee when she came to an abrupt stop. Only inches away from Freddi, she stood staring at her. Jennifer had noticed the older woman watching Freddi throughout the evening, but she was caught completely off guard by what came next.

"You're the girl in the picture!" Abby exclaimed, the coffeepot trembling slightly in her hands.

Freddi gave her a puzzled look. "The girl in the picture?"

With an eager nod, Abby glanced at Mitch, who appeared flushed and decidedly uncomfortable. "The picture in your wallet, Mitch! Remember, when I was looking at your snapshots, and I asked you about the girl with the long black hair?"

Turning back to Freddi, she regarded her with unmistakable satisfaction. "You're much prettier now, dear." Almost as an afterthought, she added, "Mitch said the two of you used to be best friends. How nice that you can be together again."

As Jennifer watched, Freddi slowly turned to Mitch with a look that was both pleased and questioning. "Yes," she said quietly. "Isn't it?"

Mitch, who seemed to have developed an acute interest in something on the floor beside his foot, remained stonily silent.

As if to rescue him from his embarrassment, Freddi smoothly changed the subject. "Mitch, have you seen anyone — peculiar — around town lately?"

Mitch looked up. "Peculiar?"

Freddi nodded. "Huge guy," she said, her tone thoughtful. "Probably six-six or more. Bodybuilder type — very muscular. He was standing several yards off from the chapel. Dressed all in black. With sunglasses," she added, frowning. "Though he couldn't have needed them by then."

Mitch shook his head. "I can't think of anyone like that in Derry." He looked at Abby. "Did you see him, Abby?"

Abby didn't seem to be listening. She

had plopped down on a small rocking chair across from Mitch and was playing with Pork Chop, a spotted cocker spaniel — one of several dogs that seemed to parade at will in and out of Mitch's cabin.

When Mitch repeated his question, adding Freddi's details, Abby's reaction puzzled Jennifer. She went ashen, and her voice trembled almost as badly as her hands. "A big man in black clothes? with sunglasses?"

"Did you see him, Abby?" Freddi prompted.

Abby didn't answer. Instead, perched on the edge of the chair, she began to hug herself, rocking forward and back as she stared out the glass doors into the darkness.

Mitch glanced from Abby to the door, then went to her. "Abby," he said softly, stooping down in front of her.

Slowly, she turned to look at him. Her expression had cleared somewhat, but her eyes were still troubled, her body rigid.

Mitch's voice was gentle as he took her hand. "Abby, what is it? What's wrong?"

Abby stared at him, her gaze strangely vacant. "Wrong?" she repeated. "Why, nothing, dear. Nothing's wrong."

Mitch studied her for a long moment.

Watching the two of them, Jennifer sensed that this had happened before.

Finally Mitch stood and helped Abby up from her chair. "We'd better get you home," he said. "It's late." He darted a look at Freddi. "I'll take you back to your car after we drop Abby at her place, if that's all right."

Freddi merely nodded and, uncoiling herself from the chair, got to her feet.

The silence in the cabin after they had gone was unsettling. Daniel broke it by bending forward and fumbling hopefully around the cookie platter. "Anything left?"

"Here." Jennifer guided his hand to one of two remaining brownies.

"Is this the last one? I'll share."

Distracted, Jennifer mumbled, "No, it's all yours."

"Something bothering you?" he asked, as if he knew there was.

"Abby. She seemed so — strange for a moment. I had the distinct feeling that she didn't even know where she was."

Finishing off the brownie, Daniel wiped his hands on a napkin and sank back against the couch again. "So — tell me about Abby."

Jennifer thought for a moment. "She's very attractive. She has this really sweet, pretty face — and her eyes are wonderful, like a china doll's. I suppose she's probably in her early to mid-sixties."

"And she troubles you."

Jennifer thought for a moment. "It's as if there's something . . . missing about her. She's warm and sweet and delightful. . . ." Uncertainly, she let her words trail off.

"But?"

Jennifer glanced away and sat staring into the cold fireplace. What *did* trouble her about Abby? For a moment tonight she had half expected the older woman to rise from her chair and go walking outside into the darkness as if someone . . . or something . . . had called to her.

With a sigh, Jennifer turned back to Daniel. "I'm not sure," she said, still troubled.

He patted the cushion beside him, and Jennifer moved closer. Pulling her into the circle of his arm, he coaxed her head against his shoulder. "So how does it feel to have spent an evening with a celebrity?" he asked.

"Freddi? Actually, it's hard to remember who she is — that she's famous, I mean. She's incredibly easy to be with, not at all what I would have expected."

"Am I right in thinking that Mitch

doesn't find it quite so easy to be with her?" he asked.

Again Jennifer sighed. "Poor Mitch."

"Poor Mitch?"

"I think his life is about to become extremely complicated."

"Ah." He nodded wisely. "The lady Gwynevere, I presume."

"There's a story there." Jennifer had always loved a good mystery. And a good mystery seasoned with a touch of romance, as seemed to be the case with this particular situation, was a combination that never failed to ram her curiosity into overdrive.

"Oh, a *story.*" Daniel grinned in anticipation.

"Exactly. You should see the way she looks at him."

"Something like the way you look at me?"

She tilted her head to glance up at him. "Well . . . yes, as a matter of fact."

"And Mitch?"

"Mitch," she replied after only a second's hesitation, "looks at Freddi like a man standing on the edge of a cliff trying to decide whether he should take a flying leap or turn and run."

"I can identify with that. That's pretty

much how I felt when I realized I was falling in love with you."

Jennifer looked at him. "By the way, Daniel, just how is it that you *know* the way I look at you?"

His smile was nothing short of smug. "Oh, I've been told."

"Gabe-the-Mouth strikes again," Jennifer said dryly.

Daniel shrugged off the reference to his brother-in-law. "No shame in a woman showing her love for her husband."

Jennifer grinned at him, waiting.

One heavy dark brow lifted in anticipation. "Don't you agree?"

"Oh, I do."

"So?"

Agreeably, she wrapped her arms around his neck.

FOUR

Squeezed snugly between Abby and Mitch in the front seat of his blue pickup, Freddi tried not to think about Mitch's closeness. More than once, however, she thought about all the times . . . so many years ago now . . . the two of them had bumped along this same deserted mountain road. It was difficult to believe that the tall, confident man behind the steering wheel was really Mitch, that she was home, and that they were together again.

No. Not *together.* Too many years of separation lay between them — almost a decade of differences and distance. The man beside her wasn't the boy she had left behind. Nothing was even remotely the same as it had once been.

Nostalgia rushed at her, deepened by the lonely silence of the night. A tidal wave of images threatened to overwhelm her — the shadowed silhouette of Mitch's profile beside her, the faint cinnamon-clove scent of the rock candy he still carried in his pocket. . . .

And his sporty blue truck. There had

been a time — so many years ago that it now seemed like forever — when she had sat on a riverbank holding hands with a lean-faced boy, listening to his solemn declaration . . . "Someday, I'm going to buy me a bright blue truck with a shine you can see your pretty face in, instead of driving you around in that ugly, old, broken-down wagon truck."

Mitch's dreams had always been incredibly simple, as uncomplicated as the boy he had been, as gentle as the man he seemed to have become. Back then her own dreams had seemed vastly more important, so much bigger and brighter. . . .

The drive to find out what lay beyond Derry Ridge had been at the heart of Freddi's dreams for as long as she could remember. She had entertained only one other ambition throughout all the years of growing up: to write, and to write so well that all the world would rush to read what she had written.

Although Mitch had pretended to understand the fury that drove her, he had never really been able to comprehend her desire to reach beyond what she already had. He had always loved the Ridge and everything it encompassed: its people, its music, its history, its heritage. While he had yearned only to become one with the mountain, Freddi had longed to separate herself from it and explore what lay beyond.

For as long as Freddi could remember, Mitch had ached to have a place of his own, a "homeplace" right here on the Ridge. And in spite of his inability to comprehend *her* need to get away, she thought she had instinctively understood *his* need to stay.

His father had deserted his teenage wife not long after Mitch was born. Before Mitch was old enough to go to school, his mother had dumped him on a relative and headed for her own "fresh start" somewhere in North Carolina, leaving Mitch to spend the rest of his childhood being passed from one indifferent aunt or uncle to another. He had never known the security, the stability, of a real home.

In contrast, Freddi had grown up under the shelter of a widowed, doting grandfather after the death of her parents in an airplane crash. Her father, the community's only veterinarian, and her mother, a Latin teacher at the high school, had left Freddi financially independent. She had marched confidently through childhood and adolescence, much loved and admittedly pampered by her grandfather.

It was no wonder she and Mitch had reached for different stars. She was glad to see that he had finally attained his dreams, or was well on his way to doing so. He deserved it all — the directorship of the new Heritage department, the doctorate he had recently completed, and the moderate success for his newly published textbook on eastern Kentucky folk music, coauthored with another instructor on campus. Along the way he had built not only his cabin home but a meaningful campus ministry as well.

Oh, Lord, why couldn't I have realized then how very small my own dreams were? They were nothing but tinsel — empty and vain, without any lasting value. . . .

Beside her, Abby spoke, rousing Freddi from her memories. "The mountain's nice at night, isn't it? So quiet and untroubled."

Freddi smiled at the older woman in the darkness. "You like it here very much, don't you, Abby?"

"Oh my, I certainly do! You'll come in and see my place, won't you?" she urged Freddi. "You can meet Peaches, too."

"Peaches?"

"Peaches," Mitch explained dryly, "is a mountain lion posing as a cat. The little

64

beast has teeth like a chain saw and claws like carpet tacks. Believe me," he said with a wry twist of his mouth, "her name is the only sweet thing about her."

"Oh, Mitch, she's only a kitten!" Abby scolded. "She just likes to roughhouse with you."

"She likes to make me bleed, you mean." He gave Freddi a conspiratorial wink, another familiar gesture from years past that made her heart skip.

The three of them sat in silence the rest of the way up the road. Both windows were down, and the night breeze, a little cooler now, felt good on Freddi's face.

The strong scent of pine and hardwood meshed with the heady odor of rich, spring-warmed earth and the fragrance of mountain wildflowers. Somewhere on the hillside a dog howled, and Freddi shivered. This late at night, the ridge was a lonesome place to be, at times forbidding in its isolated darkness.

As Mitch pulled into the gravel turnaround at Abby's cabin, Freddi suddenly realized that it was *too* dark.

"I thought you set the floodlight to turn on at nine," she said.

"I did. The timer must not have worked."

Freddi leaned forward. Draped by a shroud of darkness, the cabin was almost indistinguishable from the woods that surrounded it. Something didn't seem quite right. But what?

The door.

"Mitch —" Keeping her eyes straight ahead, Freddi put a hand on his arm.

He shot a questioning look at her, then at the darkened cabin. The sky that had been clear a short time before was now thick with clouds, the thin slice of moon no longer visible.

His eyes still on the cabin, Mitch reached over to add the pickup's overhead running lights to the headlight beams. In the tumbling roll of light that hit the front porch, the open doorway gaped like a black hole.

Abby gasped and fumbled to open the door of the truck. But Mitch flung out an arm to stop her. "No — wait!"

His gaze swept their surroundings as he leaned across Freddi and Abby to lock the door and roll up the window on the passenger's side, then his own. Still watching the cabin, he opened the glove compartment and withdrew a large crescent wrench, smacking it once against the palm of his hand.

Abby looked blankly from the wrench to his face. "Mitch? What are you doing?"

Mitch didn't answer but sat unmoving, scanning the cabin and the dark, forest-covered hillside looming behind it.

"Stay here," he finally said in a harsh whisper. "Keep the doors locked. If you need me, lean on the horn."

He put his hand on the door handle, but Freddi caught his arm. "I'll go with you."

"No!" He whipped around in the seat, repeating in a lower voice, "No. Let me take a look first. Just stay put until I come back."

He opened the door slowly, wincing at the metal's loud squeak of protest.

Freddi snapped the lock down as soon as he leaped from the truck, then watched him take the flagstone walk in quick, cautious steps. The tense silence inside the truck was broken only by her own shallow breathing and the sound of Abby worriedly cracking her knuckles.

All the way up the walk, Mitch told himself this was probably the work of the same gang of unruly teens that had been vandalizing various businesses and residences throughout the county over the past few months. Their random mischief had been witnessed on a number of occasions, but they were still freely roaming about the Ridge. They were probably responsible for shooting out Abby's security light the night before.

At the porch, he glanced around, seeing nothing. Quietly, he stepped up onto the wide planks and crossed to the open door.

He stopped, pressing himself against the porch wall. After a moment, he looked in. The wrench felt heavy in his hand. He tightened his grip on it and took one cautious step over the threshold.

The blackness of the room stopped him. His heart pounded as he fumbled for the light switch on the wall beside the door.

An immediate wash of light illuminated the room, and Mitch froze.

The seat of the couch had been slashed all the way across, its ruffled cushions tossed to the floor. Books had been spilled from the shelves beside the fireplace, some ripped from their bindings and pitched across the room. The single drawer of the petite spinet desk he had given Abby for Christmas was overturned on the floor, its contents strewn haphazardly nearby. In front of the window and beside the end table were shattered pieces of broken lamps.

In spite of the cool breeze blowing in through the open door, Mitch felt hot and sick with fury and disbelief. He took a couple of unsteady steps toward the middle of the room, his mind struggling to take in the wanton destruction.

His heart pounding, he left the room and started down the hallway toward the kitchen. He held his breath in dread as he flipped on the overhead light.

Dishes and crockery lay shattered on the handwoven rug, and half-empty cupboards gaped, their contents tossed onto the pine counter and the floor.

Mitch's head began to pound, and a chilling whisper at the back of his mind warned that he hadn't yet seen the worst. A frantic inner voice told him to run, to get out.

With his legs shaking beneath him, he climbed over the rubble on the floor and started for the bedroom. He groped his way through the darkness to the bedside table, found the lamp, and turned it on.

He moaned aloud at the violation that greeted him. His pulse thundered in his ears, and he thought he was going to be sick.

The newly stained louvered doors of the closet had been ripped from their hinges and Abby's sparse wardrobe flung to the floor. The drawers of her small bureau had been pulled out and overturned, their contents tossed helter-skelter around the room.

Mitch stepped back, turned to leave the room, then stopped.

Peaches. *Where was the cat?*

She's outside, he realized with relief. The door had been open, hadn't it? The cat had most likely dashed from the house at the first sign of the intruders.

Just to be sure, he ducked across the hall into the small bath that opened off the bedroom.

Everything here seemed normal, except for the shelves of the small linen closet. Towels and sheets lay scattered on the floor, but otherwise nothing seemed to have been touched.

As he returned to the kitchen, a renewed sense of outrage and anger burned its way past the shock and took control of his emotions. This was worse than simple teenage mischief. Abby had been robbed of her privacy, her security, her safety. In Mitch's mind, this was almost as bad as an outright attack on her person.

It occurred to him that he ought to try to sweep up as much of the debris as possible before Abby came inside. He stuck the wrench in his hip pocket, then started across the kitchen. Pushing the calico curtain to the broom closet aside, he began to grope in the darkness for the broom and dustpan.

His foot nudged something on the floor, something soft. He stopped and leaned over, his hand touching . . . something. Mitch froze, then straightened. A cold trickle of perspiration crept along the nape of his neck as he finally reached to pull the chain on the single lightbulb above the shelves.

Peaches, Abby's small, spotted cat, lay on the floor, her neck obviously broken.

Bile rose to Mitch's throat, choking him. He had to fight back wave after wave of nausea as he dropped down to his knees. He touched the cat once, his fingers trembling as he remembered all the times he had teased Abby about her harmless little pet.

He glanced at the shelf just above his head and reached for a hand towel. Gently, he covered the lifeless cat. His eyes swept the room as he struggled to think. Rage battered at him, accompanied by a stirring of fear.

Who would have done something like

this, something so mindless, so unfeeling? And to a perfectly harmless person like Abby?

He raked a hand across the back of his neck, felt his own clammy perspiration, the coldness of his skin.

He remembered then that both Abby and Freddi were still outside in the truck. Fear swept over him, and he practically ran from the kitchen down the hall toward the front door.

The two women were standing just inside the open doorway staring at the destruction in front of them. Freddi's face was a hard mask of shock and anger. Abby was pale, with the stunned look of a wounded animal.

Seeing Mitch, Freddi took a step toward him, then stopped. "We were afraid to wait any longer," she said. "We were worried something had happened to you. . . ." Her voice caught, and she met his gaze, holding it.

Mitch felt an irrational dart of relief that she was here, that he didn't have to face Abby alone. He started toward them, warning them with an upraised hand not to come any farther.

The look on Abby's face was as horrified as he had known it would be as she stood taking in the vandalism to her cabin. The bewildered gaze she turned on Mitch was imploring, a plea for him to tell her that none of this was real.

Knowing that the worst was yet to come, Mitch fumbled for words, for answers to her unspoken questions. But the only thing he managed was a steadying arm around her shoulders. When he felt Abby tremble under his touch, he tightened his grasp.

At this moment, there was nothing he could say to her, nothing he could do for her. Nothing except to get her out of the cabin, away from the horror.

With a firm hand, he began to turn her toward the door, but she stood frozen.

"Abby — you mustn't come in. Come on, let's go back to the truck." Again he tried to turn her from the room.

"But Mitch, what . . ."

"Abby, please."

"Who —" Her voice broke. *"Why, Mitch?"*

Glancing over her head, he caught Freddi's gaze and silently urged her to help him. She moved to take Abby's other arm, and the two of them managed to lead her onto the porch.

At the back of Mitch's mind, a warning sounded, chilling him with the thought that whoever did this could easily be close by, watching from the woods, waiting.

His pulse hammering, he scanned the thick, inky darkness surrounding them as they started back down the porch steps. His hand went to the wrench in his back pocket in a gesture of reassurance.

Abruptly, Abby stopped and tried to pull away. "Peaches! I can't leave without Peaches, Mitch — she'll be terrified —"

Mitch shot an agonizing look at Freddi. With a grim nod of understanding, she tightened her hold on Abby's arm. "Abby, Mitch will take care of Peaches. Let's you and I go to the truck."

Only when the three of them were safely locked inside the pickup, this time with Abby in the middle, did Mitch tell them, as gently as possible, what had happened to Peaches.

FIVE

The rain began the next morning. True to form for a Kentucky mountain rainstorm, its beginning was deceptively mild and seemingly harmless. But as a native, Freddi knew it was only a matter of hours before the drizzle would become a downpour.

She sat next to a window in the dining room of the Lodge and studied the pewter sky through light rain splashing against the glass. Maybe the gloomy weather wasn't all bad, she thought. At least the weather would provide a safe topic of conversation for her and Mitch when he arrived.

If he arrived. Freddi's suggestion that they meet for breakfast this morning had been strictly an impulse and met with awkward hesitation on his part. Still, it had been Mitch's idea to strand her at the Lodge without a car.

He had caught her completely off guard the night before with his insistence that she leave her car in the campus parking lot and let him drive her to the Lodge. When she protested, reminding him that she needed a way in to her morning workshop, Mitch

75

had faltered only a moment. "That's no problem. I'm going to Abby's place first thing in the morning to . . . take care of the cat. I'll drive on up to the Lodge afterward, and you can ride in with me."

When Freddi would have objected, he silenced her with a flat, slightly obstinate warning. "You've got no business driving that road by yourself this late. Especially after what happened at Abby's."

It *had* been late — nearly two — when they had finally gotten Abby settled in at Mitch's cabin. Daniel Kaine, with a quiet, soothing kindness, and Jennifer, with a brisk, no-nonsense manner that seemed to balance her apparent mother-hen instincts, had both been wonderfully helpful with the distraught Abby.

For her own part, Freddi had been restless throughout the night. When she wasn't sparring with herself about her feelings for Mitch, she was replaying in vivid detail the destruction at Abby's cabin. The scene had stirred nagging questions about the woman who had seemingly come from nowhere. She supposed it was force of habit for a mystery writer.

Abby intrigued her: her missing past, her lack of identity, the circumstances that had brought her to Derry Ridge. The unanswered questions surrounding the winsome Abby were too many to disregard.

Nor had she managed to shake the unsettling memory of the black-garbed behemoth standing on the campus green the night before. By the time the first gray light of morning had begun to filter through her window, a core of suspicion had cemented itself firmly in Freddi's mind: There had to be a connection between the Monster Man and Abby. Freddi had learned to trust her hunches, and —

She was yanked abruptly out of her thoughts when the double doors to the dining room swung open and Mitch walked in. At the mere sight of his lean, ambling frame, opposing forces of longing and regret began to pull at Freddi. Swallowing, she drew in a steadying breath as she watched him cross the room in her direction.

He was wearing a navy windbreaker open over a denim shirt and pleated khaki pants. The rain had tightened the curl of his hair slightly, and his dark brows were knit together in a frown that clearly said that this meeting was a bad idea.

When he came to stand in front of her, he managed a brief, unconvincing smile. "Have you already eaten?" he asked, glancing at her half-empty coffee cup.

Freddi thought he sounded hopeful. "No. I was waiting for you."

After a slight hesitation, he shrugged out of his windbreaker and hung it over the back of a chair, then sat down across from her.

"You look tired," Freddi said.

In fact, he looked a lot worse than tired. His eyes were smudged with deep shadows that hadn't been there the day before, and there was a tightness about him, a haggard expression that left little doubt as to the kind of night he'd had.

His eyebrows lifted as he shrugged and picked up a menu.

"How's Abby this morning?"

Mitch laid the menu back on the table, then pushed it aside. "Confused. Hurt. Pretty much as you'd expect. She went to work, though."

It went on that way for several minutes. As if by silent agreement, they limited their conversation to the neutral subjects of Abby, the weather, and the view from the Lodge's dining room. In between ordering breakfast and a few idle remarks about the food when it arrived, they exchanged awkward looks and uncertain smiles.

When their fingers accidentally brushed

while reaching for the cream pitcher, Mitch flinched as if he had been seared by an open flame. If their casual reminiscing happened to skirt too close to a shared memory, he simply blinked and quickly turned away.

"Have you talked to the police yet, about last night?" Freddi asked, trying to keep the conversation as impersonal as he seemed to want it.

He scowled. "For all the good it did. Will Bannon is still chief."

Freddi made a face at the memory of Derry Ridge's Chief of Police. Bannon had been threatening an early retirement for as long as she could remember. His laziness was legendary, surpassed only by his bigotry and savage contempt for "strangers." He would be hopelessly callous toward Abby's plight.

"He calls her the 'dipsy bag lady on the hill,' if that tells you anything," Mitch added resentfully, finishing off his last bite of toast.

"Bannon always was a compassionate soul." Freddi took a sip of coffee and nibbled indifferently at her sweet roll. "It's going to take some work, putting Abby's cabin in order. I'd like to help."

Mitch gave her a long, unreadable look

before glancing down at his cup. "That's nice of you, but I think I can find some students willing to lend a hand. I want to get it cleaned up as quickly as possible."

He filled both their cups from the stoneware coffeepot, then asked their waitress to bring them more cream. After the girl had again retreated, he leaned forward, locking his fingers together on top of the table.

"I just wish there was a way to put those punks out of business," he said bitterly, staring at his hands.

"Mitch, do you really believe that what happened at Abby's place was vandalism?"

He looked up. "What else?"

Freddi hesitated. "I think it might have been . . . something more."

Saying nothing, he frowned and waited.

"It seems to me that whoever tore Abby's cabin apart was looking for something."

Openly skeptical as well as puzzled, Mitch drew back a little in his chair and crossed his arms over his chest. "Like what?"

Freddi ran the tip of one finger around the rim of her coffee cup. "Most of the damage was methodical," she explained. "Oh, there was a certain amount of rage, violence — certainly killing the cat was senseless and sadistic. But the way the couch was ripped open, the desk emptied, the closets rifled —" She shook her head, meeting his gaze. "Whoever did that was after something."

His eyes narrowed. "After *what?*"

Freddi shrugged. "There's no way of knowing. Maybe he doesn't know, either. Maybe he's just looking for — whatever he can find."

"He?" Mitch lifted one brow in a dubious look.

"Probably. Somehow I think it's only one person."

He stared at her for a long time, long enough for her to grow uncomfortable under his scrutiny.

"I suppose it follows that a mystery writer is part detective, too." He made no effort to soften the scorn behind his words.

Freddi met his sarcasm with a quiet reply. "No. But I *do* spend a good deal of time around crime scenes. And police stations and courtrooms."

He seemed to relax somewhat. "That makes sense. I suppose that's why your books always ring true."

Freddi blinked in surprise. "You read my books?"

He shrugged. "Why wouldn't I?"

She returned her attention to the rim of her coffee cup. "I guess . . . I just didn't think you would," she answered softly.

Mitch shifted in his chair. "Are you serious about what you said? You think someone deliberately trashed Abby's place because they were trying to find something?"

"Yes." She leaned forward a little, lifting her eyes to his. "Mitch, what exactly do you know about Abby? Anything more than what you told me yesterday?"

He moved to pour more coffee for both of them. "No. How could I, when she knows so little about herself?"

"What about her clothes?"

"Her clothes?"

"What was she wearing when she came here? What did she have with her?"

He thought for a moment. "Until we took up a collection and bought some stuff for her, she had only one dress. It was . . . blue, I think. Faded."

"That's all?"

"That was it, other than some toiletries. And her Bible. Why?"

Freddi met his question with another. "What about a purse?"

He gave a nod of acknowledgment. "She had a purse, but it was virtually empty. No wallet, no ID. Just a couple of small pieces of jewelry and some tissue. And an empty pillbox."

Freddi mulled that over for another instant. "It doesn't fit."

"What doesn't fit?"

"That a woman like Abby would show up with no money, no clothes, no possessions — and no past."

"A woman like Abby?" His brows drew together in a questioning frown.

"Haven't you noticed a certain —" She reached for the word she wanted. "A certain *dignity* about her? A kind of understated elegance?"

For a long moment Mitch looked at her. Then a slow-dawning light of recognition rose in his eyes. "Yes," he said, nodding slowly. "I *have*. Something about the way she sits, certain ways she holds her hands, even her head —"

"Class."

At his puzzled look, Freddi repeated, "*Class*. Abby has class."

His smile was soft and faintly tender as he echoed the word. "Class . . . that's it. That fits her. Abby's . . . a lady."

"Exactly." Freddi's imagination began to roll. "So what's a lady like Abby doing on top of a Kentucky mountain without a nickel to her name or a scrap of memory about her past?"

When Mitch didn't answer, she went on. "You said the local police tried to dig up some background on her. How much of an effort do you think they really made?"

He shrugged. "I have no idea. I suppose they did what they could."

Freddi lifted her cup and drained the rest of the coffee. "I have a friend in Chicago — a PI, one of the best in the business — who would probably do some checking for us, if I asked him to."

She could almost hear the questions forming in Mitch's mind as he studied her.

"Boyfriend?" His tone was light, but his eyes were hard.

"Friend," Freddi emphasized.

His gold-flecked eyes continued to probe hers for a moment. Then he shook his head. "I don't think so."

Freddi drew back, watching him. "Why not?"

He looked away. "I'm not sure we have the right. It seems . . . almost like prying." His voice held a sharp edge when he turned back to her. "Besides, there's no money to pay someone like that. Even I know private investigators don't come cheap."

"I told you he's a friend. There wouldn't be a fee."

"He must be a *good* friend."

Unless Mitch had changed a great deal, the pointed remark and accompanying borderline sneer represented all the nastiness of which he was capable. Freddi decided to ignore the dig. "Aren't you curious enough to want to try?"

Again he glanced away. "What if there's some kind of trouble in Abby's past — something she's running away from?"

"That's a possibility. But it's also possible that there are people in her past, people who love her and are trying to find her. A husband, children — what about them?"

As she watched, he closed his eyes for an instant, then opened them, saying nothing.

"Mitch," Freddi probed quietly, "are you afraid of what we might find out?"

He turned back to her but remained silent until he had taken a long drink of coffee. "Maybe. I'd hate to see Abby hurt."

Freddi hadn't expected him to admit what came next. "Maybe I'm also a little afraid of losing her. She's become really important to me."

"That's not likely to happen. Abby adores you."

He smiled a little, and she saw a brief flash of the younger, roguish Mitch. "Yeah, it takes a certain amount of maturity to appreciate my charm."

For a long time they both continued to stare outside in silence as they watched the light, steady rain. Finally Mitch turned back to her. "Go ahead," he said.

Freddi looked at him. "What?"

"Go ahead and ask your . . . friend . . . to see what he can find out. I don't like it, but I suppose it's the right thing to do." He shot her a look. "But anything he turns up gets run by me before it gets to Abby."

Freddi nodded. "Of course."

After another brief silence, he sighed heavily. "I just wish I knew what to do with her now."

"What do you mean?"

"She can't stay alone. Not after what happened last night." Jabbing at the table with his thumb, he added, "Especially if you're right about it being deliberate."

"How do you think Abby would feel about a roommate for a few days?" Freddi didn't know what had sparked the idea, and the words surprised her as much as they seemed to catch Mitch off guard.

"A roommate?"

Freddi nodded. "Me."

She thought he was going to choke on the cinnamon ball he had just popped into his mouth. "*You?* Stay with Abby?"

"Why not?"

His face tightened. "What exactly are you up to, Freddi?" he demanded. "A new plot? You smell the makings of another best-seller, is that it?"

She bristled. "I'm not up to anything, Mitch. I'm trying to help. Is that really so inconceivable?"

He leaned forward, his eyes glinting with challenge. "Abby lives in a three-room cabin on the topside of a mountain — a mountain which, as I recall, you were never overly fond of. She doesn't own a hot tub; she doesn't even own a television set. Her idea of entertainment is crocheting afghans for one of the local nursing homes." He stopped and brought his face even closer to hers. "Not exactly the lifestyle to which you've become accustomed, is it, Freddi?" he added caustically.

Their eyes locked and held. "What exactly do you know about my lifestyle, Mitch?" she countered evenly.

He backed off a little. "Point taken. But you still haven't told me what you're up to."

His expression was more than skeptical.

It was openly hostile.

"I told you I'd planned to stay at the farm," Freddi said evenly. "But it's going to be a few days before I can settle in." Warming to her own idea, she pressed on. "If Abby would have me, it would give you a little peace of mind, wouldn't it? At least she wouldn't be alone."

"She doesn't have room."

"She has a couch."

"Not anymore," he reminded her almost viciously.

Freddi thought for a moment, then nodded. "I'll replace the couch. It can be my way of paying my keep, for however long I stay with her."

Mitch's eyes narrowed even more as he studied her with open mistrust. Then he slowly eased away, sinking back against the chair. "Freddi . . . why did you come back?"

Unprepared for his bluntness, Freddi at first attempted to skate around the truth with a weak laugh. "I thought you were the man with all the answers this week." She paused. "I'm doing a creative-writing workshop, remember?"

"I'm sure you get more than your share of workshop invitations," he said acidly, his eyes still hard. "Try again, Freddi."

Gripping the rim of her saucer between both hands, Freddi groped for an answer that would be honest but not too revealing. "I'm not sure you'd believe me."

His look never wavered. "It might take some doing, but try me."

Freddi swallowed, then looked away. Staring into the leaden gloom of the morning, she knew that it was too soon to tell him . . . everything.

"Let's just say that it was time to . . . make some changes in my life."

Uncertainly, she looked back at Mitch. His gaze was relentless, raking her face with undisguised suspicion. "What kind of changes?"

She tried a careless shrug, but it came off badly. "My life's become . . . too fast. Too fast, too frantic — too much. Even my writing is out of control. I decided to take some time for myself, do some thinking. Besides," she added quickly, before he could interrupt with another jibe, "I was homesick."

Homesick for my best friend . . . my hero . . . my love.

She watched him, anticipating more sarcasm. Anticipating anything but what came.

His eyes were still wary but no longer

contemptuous as he leaned toward her. "Freddi, are you in some kind of trouble?"

Freddi stared at him. "Trouble?"

Still searching her face with what appeared to be genuine, if guarded, concern, Mitch pressed, "Do you need help?"

He hadn't believed her. He hadn't even *heard* her. Freddi suddenly felt incredibly sad. Was she really that shallow, that untrustworthy in his eyes . . . in his memory? "No, Mitch," she said softly. "I'm not in any kind of trouble. I simply wanted to come home, that's all."

For a long time he sat silently studying her. When he finally spoke, his words pierced her heart. "Freddi, if the Ridge wasn't big enough for you when you were eighteen, it's surely not big enough for you now. Not after being where you've been, doing all you've done. Don't forget how desperate you were to get away from here."

"That was a long time ago, Mitch."

"Some things don't change. The Ridge hasn't changed, Freddi."

But I have, Mitch. . . . I have. "I was counting on that," she said softly.

He leaned back, his shoulders sinking heavily against the back of the chair. "You're really serious."

"Yes."

"It won't work, Freddi," he said, shaking his head slowly. "You'll never stay."

It has to work, Mitch. . . . The only part of me that's worth anything is somewhere back here, on this mountain . . . with you. . . .

He got to his feet so abruptly the chair collided with the wall. "We'd better go."

Freddi stood, fumbling in her purse for a pen to sign the check.

His hand covered hers just long enough to slide the check from between her fingers, and she jumped. "I'll get it," he said, holding her gaze. "We don't have to go dutch anymore." For an instant the faint smile in his eyes was unguarded and almost warm.

He took her arm as they started toward the cashier's counter. "There's a chapel service each morning at nine-fifteen," he said. "You'll have a few minutes after that before you start your workshop."

"Good," Freddi said brightly, waiting as he slipped the bills from his wallet to pay the check. "That'll give me a chance to see how Abby feels about a roommate. Will she be in chapel?"

Mitch glanced over at her and nodded, then reached for her rain poncho and slipped it over her shoulders.

Feeling his hands linger on her shoulders

for a second longer than necessary, Freddi held her breath.

"You *are* serious?" he asked quietly before dropping his hands away.

Freddi turned to face him. "Totally. In fact, I think Abby and I will have a great time together."

Mitch shook his head, drew a long breath, and again took her arm. "Why do I have the feeling you're absolutely right about that?" he muttered, leading her out of the dining room.

SIX

The man stood in the field behind the student center, his huge frame half-hidden behind a massive, gnarled maple tree. He kept off to the side just enough to have a good view of anyone going in or out of the student center building and the chapel across the parking lot.

Indifferent to the light rain, he watched Donovan follow the black-haired, foxy-looking woman up the walk and through the doors of the chapel, right behind the blind man and his wife.

He glanced at his watch. It was almost nine-fifteen.

There she was. As usual, the old ditz came at a run, bolting out the door of the student center, head down against the rain. Veering to the right, she pounded across the parking lot, then went racing up the sidewalk to the chapel. He hadn't seen her walk at a normal pace yet. She always seemed to hit the pavement running.

Watching her, a knot of pressure behind his left eye began to pound in frustration. He hadn't allowed for all the fuss this week with this — *festival,* or whatever it was. Most likely it would mean a change in the old woman's routine. From the looks of a discarded schedule he'd picked up behind the chapel, there was something going on day and night.

He resented the upheaval in his plans. He had originally intended to make his first move on her by tomorrow, Wednesday at the latest. But now it looked like the whole campus was going to be mobbed with teachers and kids most of the time. The old lady hadn't been alone for more than a few hours since yesterday.

Talk about lousy timing. He had expected to find a crackers old dame on her own — an open target. Instead, the place was swarming with students, and the old lady obviously had more people in her life than he had been led to expect. In addition to the teacher, the blind man and his wife were sticking pretty close. And apparently the savvy-looking dame with the Mercedes was part of the club as well.

His mouth twisted in a sneer as he thought of the black-haired woman. He had just about run her off the road the day before, up by the dam. If he had gotten a closer look at her, he wouldn't have been in such a hurry to waste her. Still, she seemed to be mixed up with Donovan and the old lady, so that meant he'd have to get rid of her. Later, he thought, cracking a quick smile. Something had to make this stupid job worthwhile.

The clincher was the rain. He was holed up in an abandoned storage shed, deep in a pine woods not too far from Donovan's and the old lady's cabins. He had thought it would be all he needed for a few days, but with this rain, it was probably going to turn into a cold, wet hole real fast.

A familiar crawling sensation spread over him; he could almost feel the dry, stinging rash begin to splotch his skin. Digging first at his forearms, then at his shoulders and chest, he began to carelessly rake the rash with his fingertips.

After another moment, he turned and started to walk up the incline behind the student center. Pulling his cap down a little tighter around his head, he started toward the dense forest that opened onto a rough path up the mountain. He zipped his black poncho all the way up to the collar, hunkering inside it against the rain as he trudged along the overgrown clearing through the woods.

He hated jobs like this. You planned and planned as close as you could, and then it all blew up in your face because the jerk that gave the orders hadn't done his homework.

Now he was going to have to blow at least another day or two figuring out how many others needed doing besides the old woman. He already knew Donovan had to go, but it was beginning to look as if there might be several more.

He hadn't turned up a thing at the old lady's cabin. Not that he had really expected to. He was beginning to think this whole stinking job was a waste. His blood heated just thinking about it, and he again raked his nails over his itching forearms.

Abruptly he remembered the cat he had killed the night before. He had always hated cats. There had never been less than half a dozen of them creeping around his simpleminded aunt's apartment — skinny, screeching for food, stinking up the place. He killed them off every chance he got. Remembering the one he'd wasted the night before helped to cool him down a little.

He took a swipe at some of the wet, low-hanging branches slapping him in the face. The pine needles scraped his skin as he charged his way through the woods. But despite the rain and the rash, he was feeling better.

And once the old lady and her friends were out of the way, he would feel good — real good.

Good and rich.

SEVEN

By eleven o'clock that night, Jennifer was incapable of thinking beyond a hot shower and a soft bed.

The day had turned into a marathon: workshops in the morning and afternoon, followed by a concert that evening. After the concert, the four of them had spent another two hours finishing the cleanup at Abby's cabin and helping Freddi move in.

Somehow they had also managed a frenzied trip into town and a visit to Derry Ridge's only furniture store, where they hastily purchased a new sofa bed for Abby's cabin.

Freddi's determination to buy the couch triggered what easily could have turned into a major clash between her and Mitch. Daniel, however, had mollified both of them by suggesting that he and Jennifer would like to help Abby, too. The end result was that Daniel paid half the purchase price of the couch, Freddi the other half.

At the moment, Jennifer would have settled for *any* couch, so long as it was close by and out of the rain. Hurrying up the steps of the deck, she huddled gratefully against Daniel's warmth while they waited for Mitch to unlock the cabin door.

She uttered a weary moan as Daniel pulled her under his arm and gave her a hug. "Tired?"

"I don't know which did the most damage," she admitted, "the long day or the second piece of Abby's chocolate cake."

Daniel shook his head. "You must have a real zinger of a metabolism. By all rights, you ought to look like the Pillsbury Dough Boy, the way you eat."

Too tired to counter, Jennifer waited for Sunny to lead Daniel through the now-open door, then followed.

The phone was ringing as they walked in. Mitch stopped only long enough to turn on the lamp beside the couch before starting down the hall. "I'd better get that, in case it's Abby."

After locking the door, Jennifer went to hang up their jackets in the hall closet. When she came back, she found Daniel already sprawled out on the couch, his legs out in front of him. At his feet, Pork Chop was scurrying delighted circles around Sunny who merely sat unmoving, eyeing the energetic cocker spaniel with good-natured tolerance.

Jennifer sank down beside her husband and watched the two dogs for a moment, then turned to Daniel. "I'm really glad you had that idea to help pay for Abby's couch. Now I feel as if we've done something to help her, too."

He nodded. "You like her a lot, don't you?"

"How could anyone *not* like Abby? She's precious."

"Well, I'm afraid there's *someone* out there who doesn't like her very much," he said grimly.

"Daniel, do you really think she's in danger?"

Locking his hands behind his head, he nodded. "It's beginning to look that way. Mitch told me tonight that Freddi's suspicious that there might be a connection between the guy she saw at the musical last night and what's been happening to Abby."

"I know. She told me while we were unpacking." Jennifer shivered slightly as she recalled Freddi's detailed description of the stranger in black.

"So, what do you think of the mystery lady now? It sounded to me as if the two of you were hitting it off pretty well."

Straightening, Jennifer scooted closer to

him. "Daniel, can you believe it? I actually helped *Gwynevere Leigh* unpack her luggage tonight!"

"You're really impressed with her, aren't you?" he asked after a moment.

"Of course I'm impressed. Look at what she's accomplished, and she's not even thirty years old yet."

"Her books, you mean?"

"Her books — her *life*. She's a huge success, you know. She's also beautiful and intelligent — and surprisingly nice. You'd never dream she's a celebrity, would you? She's so — genuine. And did I tell you she's a Christian?"

Daniel nodded and smiled. "A couple of times."

Jennifer looked at him. "I suppose you think I'm being childish."

Still smiling, he shook his head. "A little starstruck, maybe, but not childish."

Jennifer bit her lower lip, thinking. "I don't think it's wrong to admire someone who's accomplished as much as Freddi has."

"Hey, I'm not criticizing you. I understand." He pulled her into his arms. "I just want you to realize, though, that in a lot of ways you're more of a success than the Gwynevere Leighs of the world."

Jennifer laughed at his foolishness, and he pulled back, frowning. "I'm serious. Look at all the people in your life — the people you love and make happy. Like me. And Jason. And so many others, Jennifer. There's no index for that kind of success, but I expect it counts for a lot with the Lord. One of the things that makes you so special is your servant's heart, and I love you for it."

Jennifer studied him, lifting a hand to his bearded cheek. "What a sweet thing to say, Daniel."

He caught her hand and held it. "I mean it, Jennifer. Don't minimize the importance of everything you do. What about your family — and mine? And those little preschoolers you teach on Sunday and the people who listen to your show on the air every day and hear you sing in the choir at church?"

His words warmed her, but Jennifer couldn't help but wish that just once she could accomplish something *truly* special. Something important.

It would be enough, she thought, to excel in just one thing. Daniel and his entire family were *achievers*. Athletes and teachers, musicians and physicians, craftsmen and builders — the Kaines were a mix of all kinds of gifts and abilities. She had her music, of course, but even though Daniel told her she had an "incredible" voice, Jennifer knew the truth — that her voice was better than average but less than great. She had come to terms with that long ago.

Lately, however, it seemed that everyone around her was doing important things — things that *mattered*. Everyone except her.

The restlessness she had felt for the past few weeks had left Jennifer frustrated. What in the world did she want, after all? She had a wonderful husband whom she loved more than life, an adorable son, a good home — how could she possibly feel . . . *unfulfilled?* And yet she *did*. Unfulfilled — and guilty, guilty that she felt as she did.

"Jennifer?"

She jumped at the sound of Daniel's voice.

"Is something wrong?" He was still holding her hand, and now he gave it a gentle squeeze.

Jennifer looked at him.

"Jennifer . . . are you happy?"

Appalled that he even had to ask, Jennifer hurried to reassure him. "Oh, Daniel, of course I'm happy! How could I be anything *but* happy?"

Exactly, Jennifer . . . how could *you?*

His expression was still one of concern and uncertainty. Jennifer kissed him gently on the cheek. "Daniel Kaine, any woman would have to be a total fool not to be happy with a husband like you," she said firmly. "And I am *not* a foolish woman!"

He seemed to relax a little. "It must be me. Maybe I'm just feeling a little insecure."

Jennifer studied him, but before she could question him further, Mitch appeared in the doorway. He did not, Jennifer noted, look happy.

"I'm beginning to think this week just wasn't meant to be," he said.

Daniel apparently heard the strain in his voice. "What's the matter?" he asked, releasing Jennifer and getting to his feet.

"That was Lifestream's manager on the phone. He called to cancel the group's Friday night concert. It seems their bus wrecked just outside of Nashville last night, and three of their guys are in the hospital." He paused. "Including Dylan Gray, their lead singer."

"Oh no!" Jennifer sat forward. "How badly are they hurt?"

"Gray and the driver are listed as critical; the other fellow will probably be released in a few days."

Daniel frowned. "What happened, do they know?"

"Head-on collision. Mason said it was an ugly night. A lot of fog and heavy rain."

Jennifer saw Daniel wince slightly. Mitch's description had no doubt jarred a painful memory of a similar accident — the one in which Daniel had lost his sight.

"Apparently an elderly man went left of center and rammed into their bus," Mitch continued. He let out a long, weary sigh. "That heavy rain is headed our way, incidentally."

His left shoulder lifted in a tension-relieving gesture, then dropped. "They were the anchor event for the entire week. Now we're going to have hundreds of people expecting a Friday night concert that isn't going to take place."

"Can't you bring in someone else?" Daniel asked.

"Not on such short notice." Mitch shook his head with obvious frustration.

"Why don't you do it yourself?" Daniel suggested. "You don't have to take a backseat to anyone as a musician. Get some of the kids together and do your own concert."

Mitch stared at him incredulously.

"Come on, Dan. I play a little banjo and guitar, that's all."

"*And* a little fiddle, a little mandolin, and a little dulcimer," Daniel recited dryly.

"Yeah, well, bluegrass isn't on the program. And I'm certainly no CCM star. I couldn't begin to —"

He stopped in midsentence and turned an intent, measuring look on Daniel. After a moment he began to nod, slowly, then more vigorously.

"*You* could do it!"

"I could do what?" Daniel parroted blankly.

"The concert!" The worry that had darkened Mitch's eyes only an instant before suddenly lifted. "You're a natural."

His words tumbled out fast and sharp. "You're perfect for it. You've got a great voice — I heard you sing with your teen group at that youth rally in Clarksburg, remember? And you're absolute dynamite on keyboards. Plus the fact that you've got name recognition because of *Daybreak* and your numbers on the charts."

He stopped, a broad smile of obvious relief breaking over his features. "You'll be great!" He paused. "You *will* do it, won't you, Dan?"

Stunned by the lengthiest stream of conversation she had yet heard from the usually taciturn Mitch, Jennifer turned to Daniel for his reaction.

"You're a maniac, man. There's no way." Daniel began to shake his head firmly. "No way."

"Now wait, Dan — listen to me a minute," Mitch said urgently. "You can bail me out on this. We're talking about mostly teens and college kids here. They'll accept you just as easily as they would Lifestream."

Flicking his glance to Jennifer as if in an appeal for support, Mitch continued to press. "You've got a lot more credibility with your music than you seem to realize, Dan. Once people find out who you are — that you're the man behind *Daybreak* — well, that's all it will take. Trust me."

Daniel leaned toward Mitch in an attempt to protest, but the effusive Mitch wasn't finished. "You're exactly what I need. Where else could I get someone who could just walk on and take over on such short notice?"

"Mitchell, do you think you could just listen to me for a minute here? Please?" Daniel assumed the tone of voice he ordinarily used with Jason when he was trying to explain a very difficult point. "It's true

that I've done some stuff with my teen en-
sembles at youth rallies. *But* —" he slowed
his words, giving each one a deliberate em-
phasis — "my teens are not here this week.
It would just be me and a few instruments.
And that, my friend, does not a concert
make."

"You've got Jennifer," Mitch countered
without missing a beat. Turning to her, he
said, "Dan's told me about your great
voice. I can't wait to hear the two of you
together."

Jennifer opened her mouth to protest,
but Mitch waved off her attempt. "The
Lord *does* provide. You guys can save the
week for me."

"Mitch —" Daniel tried again.

"I wouldn't even *think* of getting up
there in front of all those people!" Jennifer
broke in. "For goodness' sake, Mitch, I
sing in our church choir — that's all!"

Daniel turned toward her. "Don't put
yourself down, Jennifer. You've got an absolutely incredible voice."

"Daniel —"

Mitch narrowed his eyes at her. "If
Daniel will do it, will you?"

"No, I will *not!* Daniel, tell him I
won't —"

"I wouldn't even consider doing it

alone," Daniel said stubbornly.

"There you are, Jennifer." Mitch's tone was solemn. "The ball's in your court."

Jennifer stared at him. Undaunted, Mitch simply shot her a boyish, thoroughly disarming grin.

"Besides," he rushed to add before Jennifer could say anything, "you can't say no without at least *praying* about it, can you? I mean, how do you know this isn't the real reason you're here this week? Maybe this is exactly why the Lord led you to Derry Ridge."

Jennifer looked at him incredulously, then turned to Daniel. Her stomach did a slow flip when she saw the frown of uncertainty on her husband's face. Mitch's outburst had obviously hit a nerve.

"All right, all right. We'll pray about it," Daniel conceded.

"Daniel!"

Daniel's shoulders went up in a shrug of helplessness. "He's right, Jennifer. We have to at least pray about it."

Jennifer gaped at him for another moment, then turned back to Mitch. Intending to level one of her sternest glares at him, she hesitated, stopped by a sudden flash of insight about the lean-faced, gentle-natured Kentuckian.

Mitch Donovan might very well possess what Daniel had rather whimsically described as the "spirit of a poet and the heart of a Christian martyr," but the gleeful, outrageous grin he now turned on Jennifer was that of an Irish sea captain about to board the enemy's ship.

Jennifer knew with a sudden, unnerving certainty that she and Daniel would be doing the concert Friday night.

EIGHT

Freddi awoke before dawn the following morning to the sound of rain pounding relentlessly on the roof of Abby's cabin.

Instantly alert, she swung her legs over the side of the sofa bed and reached for the jeans and cotton pullover she had laid out the night before. The room was cool, and she dressed hurriedly, then went to the front window to look out.

There was little to see. Mitch had replaced the security light the night before, but it was wrapped too thickly by the mountain's dense fog and a heavy curtain of rain to be little more than a feeble beacon in the darkness.

Eventually she turned away, crossing the room to turn on a lamp beside the sofa. The small living room was snug and friendly in the warm glow from the lamp. Mitch's touch was everywhere. Last night after the others had gone, Abby had pointed out to Freddi a number of pieces that he had either built or refinished: the blue milk-chair resting against the opposite wall, the double-board mantel above a

111

rebricked fireplace, the wide-planked floor he'd stained to a satin finish then accented with a multi-colored hooked rug from a local estate auction. Even most of the primitive tin and local stoneware pieces on the mantel had come from his own collection.

Smiling a little to herself as she let her gaze scan the room, Freddi reached for a treasure of her own. She picked up a small figurine music box from the lamp table where she had placed it the night before, tracing with loving gentleness the graceful lines of a barefoot young girl in a ballgown. Mounted on a pedestal meant to resemble a patch of wild flowers, the girl had long black hair and enormous eyes and was playing a wooden flute.

Mitch had given it to her on her sixteenth birthday. He had stood there, home from college just for her birthday, handsome but still too thin, watching her intently to measure her reaction. "It was so much like you I couldn't resist it," he had told her. "Classic country."

His smile had been tender but uncertain. What Freddi hadn't realized at the time was that the music box was imported porcelain. She didn't like to think about how many meals he must have skipped just to pay for it.

With great care and a feeling of sadness, Freddi turned the figurine, winding it just enough to start the music. Eyes shut, she listened to the soft, plaintive tune of "Derry Air," the song known around the world as "Danny Boy."

Freddi had slept in dozens of hotel rooms, lived in New York City, Chicago, and, for a few months, San Francisco. She had seen most of the United States, traveled to England, Ireland, Scotland, and Wales. Everywhere she went, the music box had gone with her. From place to place, year to year, night after night, she had kept it with her, and with it, the memory of Mitch. . . .

She opened her eyes, blinking away the tears as she replaced the figurine on the table. She would tuck it away in her things later, before Mitch could happen in and see it . . . but not just yet.

Leaving the room, she padded down the hall to the kitchen in her stocking feet. A dim light was glowing weakly just inside the kitchen door, enough for Freddi to find her way around. Crossing to the counter, she plugged in the coffeemaker Abby had filled the night before, then opened the cabinet above the sink to get a cup.

A brass lamp hung over the small oval table. She started across the room to turn it on but stopped at the window. Pulling the curtain back a little, she looked out, then down, in the direction of Mitch's cabin.

Last night she had been able to see his roof and one side of the deck from this same window. But not this morning. The rain-veiled darkness made for near-zero visibility. She thought she *did* see a faint glow of light coming from the cabin and stood watching it for a moment, wondering if Mitch was awake.

The coffeemaker gurgled, and she glanced over her shoulder toward the counter. When she turned back to the window, a slight movement in the distance caught her attention. She stepped closer, bringing her nose almost against the glass as she strained to see.

Off to the right, about halfway down between the two cabins, something moved. As she watched, she realized she had been wrong about the light she had seen a moment ago. It was coming not from inside Mitch's cabin but rather from the outside.

And it was moving. Suspended eerily in the darkness for several seconds, it flickered, then began to flutter away from the cabin.

With growing uneasiness, Freddi finally realized what she was seeing. Someone was down there with a lantern or a flashlight, someone who was now starting up the mountain.

Her mind raced. What kind of crazy person would be coming up the mountain before daylight — and in this kind of weather?

Instinctively she backed away, then bolted across the kitchen to turn off the night-light. With the room now in total darkness, she crept back to the window. More cautiously this time, she nudged the curtain to one side.

The light was still there, swaying and weaving its way up the mountain, toward Abby's cabin.

Freddi's throat tightened. Her eyes scanned the sky, hoping for at least a pale tracing of light, but it was still as dark as midnight.

As she watched, the light suddenly changed directions. Veering off to the right, it began to drift toward the other side of the ridge. After a few more seconds, it disappeared from her field of vision.

Chilled, Freddi stepped back from the

window, thinking about what she had seen. Somebody had been outside —

She swallowed. Somebody could have been *inside.*

She moved quickly but silently, crossing the room and fumbling through the drawers on either side of the sink until she finally located a small flashlight. Aiming the light low until she reached the wall phone beside the refrigerator, she lifted the handset and trained the flashlight on the insert card. Mitch's number was there, the first one listed.

She keyed in the number with an unsteady hand, pulling in a couple of deep breaths as she waited, praying he was all right.

Mitch answered on the second ring.

"Mitch — are you all right?"

"Freddi?" He sounded disoriented, only half awake. "What's wrong?"

"Mitch, listen to me — are you awake? I saw something — somebody — outside your cabin."

"What?" His tone was gruff but alert. "When?"

"A few minutes ago. I was in the kitchen, looking out the window, and I saw a light. At first I thought it was coming from inside your cabin, but then it started moving, coming up the mountain. Whoever it was came about halfway up and then headed west."

There was silence for an instant, then, "Are you sure?"

"*Yes*, I'm sure! That's why I called you."

"That's all you could see — a light?"

"It's too dark to see anything else."

"All right," he said after another brief pause. "I'll have a look." He stopped. "You and Abby are both OK?"

"We're fine. Abby's still asleep. Mitch? Be careful."

He grunted something unintelligible and hung up.

Mitch shrugged into his clothes and hurried downstairs, almost colliding with Dan in the living room.

"Sunny barked a couple of times a few minutes ago," Dan explained. "I took her out of the bedroom before she could wake Jennifer. She's settled down now," he added. "I don't know what she heard."

Suddenly Mitch realized that Pork Chop, too, must have been restless in the night. The cocker had been on the couch when Mitch went to bed, but he had moved upstairs to Mitch's bedroom sometime before Freddi's phone call.

Mitch waited until Dan and Sunny returned to the guest room before going outside. Dan would have insisted on going with him, and there was no point in his getting drenched, too. Besides, he felt no particular concern about whatever Freddi thought she had seen. She had always looked for the weird stuff first, before seeking a natural explanation. Chances were she had seen the flashlight of a stranded motorist or maybe even the reflection of someone's headlights. He expected to find nothing outside.

Twenty minutes later he was behind the wheel of the Ranger, heading up the mountain toward Abby's place. He had seen nothing during his ten-minute search that looked suspicious. There *had* been a sunken dip of mud not far from the back porch that looked as if someone might have slipped or skidded, but with the ground so spongy, there was no telling what might have caused it. No point in jumping to conclusions just because Freddi was feeling skittish.

Besides, who would be fool enough to go traipsing around in this miserable weather before daylight?

Someone who didn't want to be seen. . . .

He tried to push the nagging thought

away. He was cold, still sleepy, and mildly irritated with Freddi for getting him out of bed in the first place. He also had a dull headache that was growing worse by the minute.

His headlights were nearly useless in the fog, and the windshield wipers couldn't keep up with the downpour. By the time he pulled into the turnaround at Abby's cabin, he was gritting his teeth with tension.

Pulling up the hood of his warm-up jacket, he leaped from the truck and made a dash for the porch. Freddi opened the door before he could knock. "Give me your jacket," she whispered as he stepped inside.

Mitch shook his head. "I'll put it in the bathroom so it can dry out. Is Abby still asleep?"

She nodded. "There's coffee in the kitchen."

As soon as he walked into the kitchen, she poured milk into a steaming mug of coffee and handed it to him, then turned to refill her own cup.

Mitch leaned against the counter, watching Freddi, his mouth going dry in spite of the coffee. Her hair was piled carelessly on top of her head, loosely secured with some sort of foreign object that resembled a twisted knitting needle. Her nose was shiny, her eyes still smudged with sleep. She looked scrubbed, innocent, and extremely young.

She was wearing some kind of soft-looking cotton shirt — pink — and an old pair of jeans. No shoes, just socks. He found himself wondering if she still hated shoes. Did she go barefoot in her apartment in Chicago? Freddi had always detested anything that restricted her movement. Uncomfortable shoes, tight clothing, even gloves had been odious to her.

"Mitch?"

Embarrassed, Mitch realized he'd been staring. "Sorry. It takes me a while to wake up."

"I asked if you found anything."

He shook his head. "Nothing." He took another sip of coffee, then went to sit down at the table.

She followed, scooting into a chair directly across from him.

"So — do you think someone was watching your cabin?"

He saw the familiar intensity in those wide gray eyes, could almost hear the gears grinding in that imagination of hers. "In this rain? More likely it was someone

120

stranded on the road, looking for a telephone."

"Did you pass anyone on your way here?"

"No, but they could have been farther up."

Her eyes met his over the rim of her coffee cup. "You don't really believe that."

"I *do* believe it. Give it up, Freddi," he said, suddenly impatient with her. "You're not going to find any new plot ideas on the Ridge."

She seemed unruffled by the dig. "Oh, I don't know. I'd say this one is beginning to show a lot of promise."

"Such as?"

She smiled at him. "One: A weird-looking stranger shows up on the Ridge — for no apparent reason. Two: Someone shoots out Abby's security light — for no apparent reason. Three: Unknown subject rips up Abby's cabin and kills her pet cat — for no apparent reason. Four: Someone waving a flashlight sneaks away from your cabin in the middle of a predawn downpour — for no apparent reason. . . ."

He lifted a hand to stop her. "All right, all right. We've got some stuff that's out of the ordinary."

Neither of them said anything for a few

moments. Finally, Freddi got up and took both their cups to the counter for a refill. He watched her, grudgingly admitting to himself that coincidence couldn't possibly cover all the unexplained events of the past two days.

"So what's your point, Freddi-Leigh?" The familiar combination of her two names into one slipped out before he could stop it. It was a nickname he had given her years ago, a teasing endearment he no longer had the right to use.

Apparently, she hadn't noticed. With smooth, unhurried movements, she poured fresh coffee and returned to the table.

"My point," she said evenly, "is that Abby may be in a great deal of danger." Her eyes met his and held. "And if I were writing this story, your involvement with Abby would place you in jeopardy right along with her."

Startled, he almost laughed. But she was completely serious. Wearily, Mitch combed the damp hair at the back of his neck with his fingers. How could his life, so orderly and routine only a few days ago, suddenly become so complicated?

It would be easy to blame Freddi, but what good would it do?

At the touch of her fingers on his wrist,

his head shot up.

"Mitch? You look exhausted. Why don't you go back to your place and try to get some more sleep?"

He shook his head, unable to drag his eyes away from the long slender fingers touching his skin. "It's too late. I'd just feel worse the second time up."

She withdrew her hand, and, for an instant, Mitch wanted to recapture it, pull her closer.

Abruptly he stood, pushing his chair back to the table before downing the last of the coffee. "I'd better go."

Freddi rose from her chair and took his empty cup to the sink. "Is there a photography lab on campus?"

He nodded. "In Fletcher Hall — the language arts building. Why?"

She came back to the table. "What about a fax machine?"

Again he gave a small nod. "In the administration office."

"If I can reach Henderson this morning — that's the PI I told you about — he's going to want photographs." She shrugged. "I've got a picture of our man in black; I took it the other evening at the musical. If Abby will let me, I'll take a couple of shots of her this morning. I'd like to get them developed as soon as possible and fax them to Chicago."

"That shouldn't be any problem. If you give me the film this morning, I can get someone to develop it before noon."

"Great." She hesitated. "Mitch? I'm only trying to help. You *do* understand that, don't you? I *like* Abby."

Carefully avoiding her gaze, Mitch managed a weak smile. "That's good. She's really enjoying having you here."

"I wish you were."

For a moment he thought he'd only imagined it, that she really hadn't said it. He took a step away from her, then stopped, willing himself to meet her eyes.

He wasn't sure what he was looking for as he searched her face. He only knew there was something new in her eyes, something that hadn't been there when they were younger. A quiet kind of strength, a peace, a composure that pervaded her every word, her every gesture.

It almost made him angry, this unfamiliar . . . *quietness* about her. She had walked back into his life without warning, plunging him heart-deep into a backwash of painful memories and broken dreams. And when she grew tired of whatever game she was playing at the moment, she would walk *out* of his life again, leaving him to drown in the current she'd set in motion. It would be just like before: Freddi would go, and he would stay. Alone.

In a frantic effort to head off the anxiety rising in him, Mitch began to talk as they headed for the living room. He told her about Lifestream's accident, about his concern over the approaching Friday night concert, about his plea to Daniel for assistance.

"Do you think he'll do it?"

"He promised to tell me this morning." Mitch fished his keys out of his pocket as they walked into the dimly lighted living room. "I don't know what I'll do if he decides not to —"

He stopped, staring in disbelief at the table next to the sofa.

Pressure constricted his chest, then moved to his throat, choking him. Unable to move, unable to speak, he stood there, his eyes locked on the music box. All the shattered pieces of their past, all the dusty, elusive dreams they had shared together, seemed to rise slowly from the ashes.

Stiffly, he took a step toward the table, then another. Finally, he reached for the music box, touched it, picked it up, and studied it.

"I . . . was showing it to Abby last night," Freddi said in an unsteady voice. "I meant to put it away . . . later."

Mitch tried to swallow, but the fist was still lodged in his throat. He wanted to hold her. He wanted to shout at her.

"It still plays," she said, her words little more than a whisper.

Finally Freddi moved toward him, reaching for the music box. He glanced down at it once, then handed it to her.

Taking it, she wound it very slowly, lifting her face to his and smiling a little as the music began to chime.

Emotion swelled in him, threatening to explode. He started to touch her, even while his mind shouted its warning. *Don't . . . this is just a diversion for her. . . . Don't set yourself up for the pain again.*

She was only inches away from him, and he reached for her. His hand went to her hair, then hesitated when she closed her eyes. He lifted one long, silken strand, wrapped it around his fingers, then watched it slowly fall free.

Her eyes opened, traveling over his face, and he almost reeled at the memories he saw reflected there. For a moment the rain beating down on the tiny cabin became his heartbeat, drumming the past back into

126

existence, crashing through every wall of defense he had erected over the years.

"I have to go now," he blurted out inanely.

Freddi hesitated only an instant, regarding him with a level, measuring gaze. "I'll get your jacket," she said finally.

When Mitch walked out onto the porch, she followed him. It was still raining, but a weak gray light was now creeping over the sky.

"Have there been any reports on the river yet?" she asked, hugging her arms tightly to her body.

"No. They'll probably start coming in this afternoon." He glanced into the downpour, avoiding her gaze. "You might want to keep an eye on Abby once they start issuing the flood warnings. She has a thing about the river. You may have to reassure her."

At her questioning look, Mitch explained. "She doesn't like the river. She won't go near it. I'm not sure why."

"Some sort of phobia?"

He shrugged. "Maybe. She likes to keep her distance from it, that's for sure."

Still averting his eyes, he stepped off the porch. "Is it all right if Abby rides in with you this morning?"

"Of course."

"She usually goes in around seven, but not today. Let her sleep for a while and come in with you at nine. I'll tell the other ladies in the cafeteria."

Back inside the Ranger, he slid the key into the ignition and started the engine, waiting for it to warm up before pulling out. As he watched, Freddi waved, then stepped back inside and closed the door.

Mitch put the truck in gear and started down the mud-slicked mountain road, the music box's refrain playing in his mind and tugging at his heart.

NINE

Huddled inside his poncho, the man perched cross-legged on a blanket in the back of the van. The blanket was already wet from his drenched clothing, and the poncho was next to worthless for warmth. Late last night he had abandoned the ramshackle storage shed and taken refuge in the van. It would provide better shelter from the rain than the drafty, mud-floored shed.

There had to be vans all over the place in a hick college town like this; no one was going to pay any attention to one more. Besides, once he was done with the old ditz and her friends, he'd be out of here.

In spite of the miserable wet chill of the morning, his skin felt hot, almost feverish from the rage and frustration simmering inside him. The skin rash was worse than it had been for years; his left eye was infected again — probably because of the weeds he'd been tramping around in; and his gut was on fire from all the acid he was churning.

Scowling, he glanced around the van's dark interior. Here he sat, a rich man by anybody's standards, with three foreign bank accounts. He should be staying at a first-class hotel — he could take his pick — instead of hunkering out here in the woods like some homeless creep.

He rotated his shoulders and neck sideways to relieve the stiffness. At the same time he reminded himself why he was putting up with this garbage. Big bucks. He already had the first installment, and he stood to collect twice that much once he finished things here. The jerk who was financing the whole thing had accused him of messing up the first time, but he had straightened him out real quick.

The man dabbed at his eye with a clean handkerchief. Taylor hadn't flapped his mouth for long. It had taken only a couple of minutes to make the little wimp understand the facts. This week was nothing more than a loose end that needed to be tied off. He was doing it because *he* wanted to, not because some pencil-pushing lightweight was leaning on him.

He would finish the job for the rest of the dough and for his own satisfaction. And since he'd have to waste a few others besides the old lady, this week just might not be all grief. Maybe he'd get some laughs out of it after all.

He usually did.

Abby was having the dream again.

Her bedroom . . . the entire cabin . . . was filled with dark water. Cold water, black, opaque, and inhabited by . . . things . . . things that didn't belong . . . people she didn't know . . . eyes following her, glaring at her, accusing her . . . guns . . . and blood . . . blood-filled water . . .

Then came the shadow, an enormous black shadow rising up from the water. No, not a shadow, a man . . . a mammoth hulk of a man with white hair and black clothes, black like the water . . .

He was struggling, grappling with another man, a man in a white shirt. She knew this man — he was good; he cared about her. There was a girl between them, a pretty young girl with a blond ponytail and pink tennis shoes. . . .

Abby tried to scream, to warn them about the man with the gun. . . . They were going to get hurt. She opened her mouth and screamed and screamed, but she had no voice. She tried to run, to warn them, to help, but her legs were so heavy and all she could do was float . . . float in the water. . . .

She heard the explosion and tried to

scream again, but the black water choked off her voice, filled her throat and her lungs. . . .

Blood . . . the water was turning to blood. A white shirt drifted by, stained with red . . . then a pink tennis shoe . . . and another. . . .

Now beyond her she saw the man, the one with the gun. He was in the water, raging like a mad sea monster. Blood on his shirt, on his face, in his hair. He grabbed her legs, pushed his face close to hers. . . .

His eyes . . . he had no eyes. . . .

She screamed, and this time the sound finally ripped free from her throat as she shot up and forward in bed.

Arms went around her, holding her close. A voice — a gentle voice — said kind, soothing things to her, warming her from the cold, icy terror in which the dark water had wrapped her.

It was Freddi, Mitch's Freddi. Freddi was here. The water was gone. Abby told her about the dream, and Freddi held her until she was warm again.

TEN

"I've been wanting to ask you this ever since we met," Jennifer said, finally giving in to her curiosity. "How in the world did you get a nickname like 'Freddi'?"

Driving with one hand on the steering wheel, her left arm on the ledge of the door, Freddi glanced over at her. "Mitch gave it to me." She laughed softly. "He always said I was too much of a tomboy for a name like 'Gwynevere.' "

They were on their way back to the cabins after a brief trip to the small shopping center just outside of town. Some toiletries for themselves and groceries for Abby filled several bags in the backseat.

Turning off the main highway onto the narrow, snakelike road that scaled the mountain, Freddi shifted to low gear. "You and I have the same name, you know."

Jennifer shot her a questioning look.

" 'Gwynevere' — in a variety of spellings — is an old Welsh name," Freddi explained, turning her gaze back to the road. "It evolved into several different forms over the centuries. One is 'Jennifer.' Another is 'Winifred.' Mitch found out about that one and dubbed me 'Freddi.' It stuck all the way through school."

"The two of you went to school together?"

"Mm-hm. Well, in a way. Mitch is four years older than I am, but he was always . . . around. I really *was* a tomboy," she said, shooting Jennifer a quick smile, "forever getting myself into situations I couldn't get out of. Mitch just always seemed to be there to bail me out. Over the years he settled into a role somewhere between big brother and guardian."

"That would be nice," Jennifer said. "I have two brothers, but they're both younger. I often wondered what it would be like to have an older brother who'd take care of *me* for a change."

"I used to daydream about having a whole houseful of brothers and sisters," Freddi said. "My parents were killed in an airplane crash when I was in elementary school, and a couple of years later my grandmother died. That left just Grandpa and me. I loved having Mitch hover over me — except when he got too bossy, of course — but my grandfather wasn't keen on the arrangement. He never approved of Mitch."

Jennifer raised her eyebrows in surprise. How could anyone disapprove of Mitch Donovan?

Freddi grimaced when the Mercedes bounced over a huge pothole, shooting muddy water into the air.

"Grandpa was a good man," she went on, turning the windshield wipers on high, "but he had an almost obsessive sense of family pride. He could trace his ancestors all the way back to the original Kentucky settlers, and he had a real problem with people like the 'Do-nothing Donovans,' as he called them."

She glanced over at Jennifer. "He got worse when Mitch and I started dating. He didn't actually forbid us to see one another — he just made life miserable for Mitch every time he came around."

"But he continued to come?" Jennifer prompted. She could hardly wait to tell Daniel that she had been right about the romance between these two.

"Oh, yes," Freddi said with a reminiscent smile. "In his own way, Mitch was a match for Grandpa. At least in terms of stubbornness."

Pulling onto the gravel drive in front of Mitch's cabin, she put the car in park and let the engine idle. "Grandpa was never able to see the goodness in Mitch," she said softly, staring out the window. "He was so hung up on what most people *think* is important that he never looked quite far enough to see what *is* important."

Jennifer nodded. "I guess we all do that sometimes."

"Sure we do. That's why I left the Ridge."

Jennifer turned to Freddi and saw the wistful look in her eyes.

"I grew up restless," Freddi said, sinking back against the car seat as she continued to gaze out the front windshield. "I can't remember a time when I didn't want to escape the Ridge, to go — exploring. I just *knew*," she said with a humorless smile, "that there were all kinds of wonderful, exciting things waiting for me on the other side of this mountain. And I was determined to find every one of them. Career, success, excitement — I wanted it all. Everything Derry Ridge couldn't offer."

"And you found it?"

Freddi met her eyes for a long moment, then looked away. "I found it. But a few months ago I began to realize that I had lost far more than I'd found."

"And that's why you came back?" Jennifer studied Freddi's profile, puzzled by the unhappiness she sensed in the lovely young woman.

"Nothing seemed important to me any longer," Freddi answered. "I had always been restless, unsettled — but this was different. Nothing satisfied me, nothing mattered to me — not even my writing. I felt as if . . . as if I had no *reality* in my life. Everything had become so artificial — so *plastic*."

There was no self-pity or resentment in her words, merely a quiet steadiness as she went on. "For the first time in — too long — I began to really pray." She looked at Jennifer. "Until then I'd only been giving lip service to God. My writing had always come first — always. Everything else took second place."

As Jennifer listened, she began to sense that this was the first time Freddi had actually talked through her feelings. Her words were so simple and sincere that it was almost as if she were speaking to herself.

"I realize now that I was passing through a kind of crisis in my faith, a turning point. I was forced to face the truth about myself: the center of my existence had never been Christ, even though I had been a believer since I was a little girl."

Her gaze grew distant and more contemplative. "It was a devastating time for me. I was brought to a place of painful, raw honesty about what I believed and why I believed it. Gradually I began to realize that Christ had been my Savior for years — but I hadn't wanted him as my *Lord*. He had never," she added in a voice that was little more than a whisper, "really been *first* in my life."

Freddi was silent for another moment. Finally she spoke, and her words arrowed straight to Jennifer's heart.

"You see, I had to get to the place where Jesus was enough. I had to reach the point where I could say, and mean it with all my being, that if I lost everything — my writing, my success, my health, *everything* — he would be enough."

Shaken, Jennifer suddenly glimpsed a different Freddi. Or was she simply seeing the *whole* Freddi? A lonely, wounded young woman, a woman whose eyes held yesterday's sorrows and no small measure of pain. But beyond that she sensed the very essence of peace, a peace that came only from what Daniel called the "sufficiency of Christ."

Somewhere at the back of her mind, an uneasy question began to form, a question about her own peace. Could it be that she had allowed her feelings of inadequacy, her recent frustration and dissatisfaction, to invade that peace? Had she, like Freddi, forgotten that Jesus was enough?

But she *had* given the Lord first place in her life, a long time ago.

Then what accounted for the increasing feelings of discontent nagging at her?

Freddi's voice broke into her thoughts. "I can't believe it's after five already. We're going to have to hustle to make the concert tonight."

Jennifer glanced at her watch and groaned. "I promised to start dinner for Mitch! And I wanted to call and check on Jason, too." Collecting her purse, she turned to Freddi. "You and Abby are still coming for dinner, aren't you?"

"I'll drop Abby off, but I'm not staying. In fact, I think I'm going to skip tonight's concert too; I've got some things I want to do at the farm. By the way," she added dryly, "what's this I hear about you and Daniel doing a concert of your own Friday night?"

Jennifer made a face. "I had no idea Mitch could be such a bully," she cracked. "I can't believe he actually talked Daniel into this."

"You'll be super," Freddi assured her, smiling. "I'm glad you're doing it."

"*Daniel* is doing it," Jennifer corrected, opening the door. "I'll be in the front row, rooting for him."

Freddi grinned at her. "Somehow I think your husband may have other ideas."

Jennifer started to get out, then turned back. "Are you going to need any help tonight? I could go with you."

Freddi shook her head. "It won't take long. I just want to move a few things upstairs in case we get water."

"Water?"

Freddi nodded. "This is a flood district. It's easy to forget about it up here —" she inclined her head toward the upper part of the mountain — "but the farm is too close to the bottoms for comfort. The house has never taken much damage, but the first floor *has* had water a couple of times."

"You're not going to try to move furniture?"

"No, just some small stuff I'd hate to see ruined. I can prop most of the furniture up off the floor."

"Mitch will be disappointed if you don't stay," Jennifer said without thinking.

Freddi straightened in the seat, waiting for Jennifer to get out. "Most likely," she replied with a rueful smile, "Mitch will be relieved."

Five minutes later, Jennifer was appraising the contents of Mitch's refrigerator. When the telephone rang, she answered it with one hand, reaching with her free hand to set a plastic container of lettuce on the butcher-block counter.

It was Freddi. "Jennifer, is Abby there?"

"Abby? No. At least I don't think so. I've been in the kitchen ever since I came inside, but I'm fairly certain she's not here."

"She's not here either."

Jennifer glanced through the open doorway into the hall. "Hold on a minute, and I'll check the rest of the cabin." She laid the handset down on the counter.

After finding no sign of Abby anywhere in the cabin, Jennifer picked up the extension in Mitch's bedroom. "She's not here, Freddi. Maybe she went back to the campus for something."

There was a pause. "Mitch told her not to go anywhere alone."

"Do you think we should call him?"

Again Freddi hesitated. "Would you mind looking around outside? I'll do the same. If neither of us finds her, then I'll call the campus." She paused. "Did Mitch give you any idea what time he planned to come back to the cabin?"

"About six. He and Daniel were going to meet with a few students in the choir and try to put together a backup ensemble for Friday night. Listen, I'll go outside right now. I'll call you back —"

"No, if I don't find her in the next few minutes, I'll come down. Otherwise I'll call you."

Jennifer grabbed her rain jacket and exchanged her dress shoes for a pair of boots, then headed for the back door.

On the deck, she glanced around, then hurried down the steps into the yard, starting for the garage at the rear of the cabin.

It was raining again. She pulled up the hood of her jacket and dashed across the walk to the garage. Through the window that ran the length of the garage door, she could see nothing but a few tools hanging on a pegboard and a couple of spare tires leaning against the far wall.

She scanned her surroundings. Mitch's backyard was actually part of the mountain. He had cleared less than an acre directly from the slope, and his lot line merged naturally with the tree-covered hillside. A small white barn sat directly across from the garage, separated by only a few feet of gravel.

Jennifer raced across the gravel to the front of the barn, tugging the zipper of her jacket up as she went. The door was locked. She went around to the side, her feet sinking a good inch into the mud.

Mitch could have used a little gravel over here, too, she thought wryly.

She cupped her hands around her eyes and tried to see through the narrow, mud-splashed window on the side wall of the barn. It was dark inside, and the window was filthy. She squinted, waiting for her eyes to adjust. She could just barely make out the dim shapes of a lawnmower and a bicycle resting against the wall. A workshop bench cluttered with power tools stood against the far wall.

Finally, she decided to go back inside the cabin in case Freddi should call. There was still no sign of Abby.

She started toward the cabin, then stopped. Out of the corner of her eye off to her right she saw something move. A man in a black, full-length poncho was trudging resolutely up the mountain. He was ten or twelve yards away, his back to Jennifer.

Her breath caught in her throat. It had to be the man Freddi had described to them. There was no mistaking someone his size.

He was walking fast, his legs covering the rise in giant steps. Jennifer hesitated only a moment before moving. She raced across the graveled section of the yard and dipped in among the trees, taking care to stay concealed as she began to edge her way up the mud-slicked hillside.

The man was fifty yards up the mountain from her by now, but Jennifer still had a clear view of his back as he continued to climb. The wind had picked up and was slashing through the trees, hurling the rain with a force that made her face sting. Her heart was pumping hard, more from fear than exertion. She knew she ought to go back, but she was intent on seeing where he went.

About halfway up to Abby's cabin, where the woods broke into a narrow clearing for a few feet, he suddenly turned left and began to jog, his head down against the wind-driven rain.

Jennifer tried to increase her own pace, clutching at tree branches to keep from losing her balance as she climbed the slippery incline. She had to duck her head every few seconds to protect her face from the slapping tree limbs. Her lungs fought for air, and she veered left, straining to keep the man in sight.

The distance between them was rapidly widening. In order to keep him in view, she was going to have to sacrifice the refuge of the woods and break into the clearing. It would mean leaving herself open, risking his seeing her, but she was going to lose sight of him otherwise.

Her chest was on fire, the palms of her hands raw and wet. In a split-second decision, she broke forward, leaving the cover of the woods for open ground.

The man was almost out of sight. Jennifer began to run, but the mud sucked at her feet, pulling at her, slowing her pace.

Unexpectedly, the man slowed, then turned and started toward the edge of another wooded area, heading toward a dilapidated, unpainted storage barn nearly concealed by the woods. A black van was pulled in close to it, its front half nosed in among the trees.

Jennifer stopped, watching. The man went directly to the back of the van, unlocked it, and opened the doors. He raised one leg to climb inside, then stopped, his head snapping around as if he had heard something.

Jennifer caught her breath as he stood

scanning his surroundings. Below a black shooter's cap his face was pasty, his eyes concealed by dark glasses.

She tried to dart away from the clearing and back into the trees before he could see her, but as she bolted toward the woods her foot slipped in the mud. Her ankle twisted hard, and she went down, pitching forward between two enormous pine trees. She fell on her side and shoved a fist against her mouth to keep from crying out.

When she caught her breath, she realized that she wasn't hurt, only stunned and badly jarred. Praying that the man hadn't seen her, she scrambled to her feet and, half sliding, half running, fled down the side of the hill.

She heard tree branches slapping behind her.

He had seen her. . . . He was coming after her.

Mindless of the pain now, she grabbed limbs with hands already bloody, choking on the taste of her own terror as she heard the thrashing sounds closing in on her.

Then, without thinking, she whipped around to look behind her and lost her balance. She skidded into a tree and went down, hard enough to knock the breath from her.

Hot pain stabbed at her shoulder, and she leaned back against the tree, exhausted and disoriented.

He was coming after her. . . .

She had to get up, get away. Now, before he reached her. . . .

He was close, so close she could hear the sound of his footsteps.

Dear Lord, help me get away from him. . . . Please, get me out of here. . . .

"Jennifer!"

Jennifer opened her eyes to see Freddi dart out from between two trees and come running toward her. The hood of her raincoat had fallen away, and her hair was a wet black cap hugging her head.

She grabbed Jennifer's shoulders. "What happened? Are you all right?"

Shaking, Jennifer tried to form words but managed only a choked sob.

Freddi's hands tightened on her shoulders. "Jennifer, are you hurt?" she asked, her voice urgent.

Jennifer shook her head. "I thought you were him. . . ."

"Who? You thought I was *who?*"

"The man you saw on campus . . . at the concert. . . ." She couldn't stop shaking. "He was behind the cabin," she explained. "I tried to follow him, to see where he went. I thought he was coming after me."

Freddi held on to her, at the same time scanning the woods. "He was *here?* You saw him?"

Jennifer stared at her. "We have to get out of here! He may have seen me!" She strained, pulling free of Freddi. *"Hurry!"*

Again Freddi grabbed her arm, holding her as they ran.

Once Jennifer stumbled and Freddi caught her, helping her down the muddy incline, supporting her with one arm while shoving tree branches out of their way with the other. "Come on, let's get to the car."

"But Abby —"

"Abby's at the cafeteria," Freddi grated, her breath coming in gasps as they scurried the last few yards down the hillside.

The back of Mitch's cabin came into view, and both women surged forward, breaking out of the trees and racing across the gravel as fast as they could.

Freddi pulled her keys from her coat pocket, hurriedly unlocking the door on the passenger's side. Jennifer reached across the seat to unlock the other door, and Freddi jumped in behind the steering wheel. She threw the switch on the automatic door lock, then turned to face Jennifer.

"You're bleeding," she said shortly, her eyes hard.

Dazed, Jennifer glanced down at her palms.

Freddi opened the glove compartment, found a light-colored scarf, and wrapped it around Jennifer's hands. "Keep that on until we get to the campus."

She slammed the key into the ignition, waiting only an instant for the powerful engine to roar to life. She shifted hard into reverse and skidded out of the driveway, throwing gravel as she careened onto the road.

In spite of the blistering pain now burning her hands, Jennifer felt her mind finally begin to clear. "Abby's all right?" she asked, looking over at Freddi.

"She's fine. I talked with Mitch. Apparently someone called while we were in town and asked her to come back to the cafeteria and help with desserts for tonight. Mitch drove up to get her but didn't think to leave a note."

"How did you know where to find me?"

"I didn't," Freddi said, keeping her eyes on the road. "I came down to tell you about Abby after I talked with Mitch, and when I couldn't find you I went around back. I saw footprints a couple of places, some of them too big to be yours. I got worried. Then I heard you running and tried to follow the sound." She glanced over at Jennifer. "What happened?"

The heater began to purr with warm air, and little by little the vise in Jennifer's chest eased. She drew a deep breath and, huddling against the door, described to Freddi the harrowing events of the last half hour.

Throughout her entire account, she kept her eyes closed. She had seen enough of the mountain for one day.

ELEVEN

He had been watching the teacher's cabin for over an hour. Slouched down behind the steering wheel of the van, which he had parked in a dense grove of trees several yards below the cabin, he was far enough away that no one else would see him — but close enough that he could see anyone entering or leaving.

They were all inside. The old ditz had showed up with the good-looking woman in the Benz no more than five minutes ago. If the routine was the same as the night before, they would leave for the campus in another hour or so.

He was still trying to figure out the connection between the dark-haired dish and the old lady. According to the program he had picked up, she was some big-deal writer from Chicago, back in her hometown to do a workshop. So why was she playing roomies with the old woman?

He was beginning to wonder just how much squawking the old bag had done. One thing for sure, he was going to up his price when he got back. In the beginning he had hired on for three hits, tops. A week ago he thought he had it down to one — the old woman. Now it looked like he still had to take care of her plus at least four others — the teacher, the writer, the blind man, and his snoopy wife.

What was her name — it was on the program — *Kaine. Jennifer Kaine.* Did she know he had seen her this afternoon, up there in the woods?

He grinned, his eyes still fastened on the cabin. He could have offed her right there in the clearing if he'd wanted to. Dumb broad left herself wide open. He could have snapped that scrawny neck of hers with one hand. He didn't need a piece to take care of the likes of her.

But that wasn't his plan. He had no intention of leaving any evidence behind.

All that was left now was to do the job and get out. He had wasted enough time on these hicks. Fast and easy, that's how it was going to be. He wouldn't try to take them out one at a time. All he needed was a can of gasoline.

Five people, one cabin, one fire. Piece of cake. No, make that *four* people. He had other plans for *Gwynevere.*

He shook his head, grinning. Even her name was classy.

He looked at his watch. Almost six-fifteen.

When he looked back at the cabin, the door was open. The teacher walked out on the deck with the writer. They talked for a minute — Donovan looked mad about something — then they walked the rest of the way out to the driveway.

The teacher opened the door of his pickup and reached inside for something, then turned and handed what looked like a letter to the woman. They fussed at each other a few more minutes; then the woman got in the Mercedes and backed out.

Catchside waited until the teacher went back inside the cabin before starting the van and pulling out.

He stayed a safe distance behind the Benz all the way down the mountain. When she reached the intersection to the highway, instead of turning right and heading toward campus, she turned left.

Where was she going?

He sat at the intersection long enough for a couple of other cars to get between him and the Benz, then pulled out and started down the highway after her.

Wherever she was going, she was alone. That's all he needed to know.

Staying behind a red Buick and a

Toyota, he continued to keep the Benz in view. This stretch of road was straight and level enough that he could keep her in sight with no problem.

About a mile up, the Toyota turned off onto a dirt road, leaving only the Buick between him and the Mercedes. He eased up on the gas pedal a little and turned his wiper blades on high. The rain was coming down harder than ever.

Just ahead of the Buick, two kids on bicycles bumped onto the road from a driveway. Both of them had on yellow rain slickers with hoods and carried newspapers in their bike baskets. They edged far enough into the right lane that the Buick had to pull back fast, cutting his speed by half.

Catchside uttered an oath and tapped his brake. The Benz was already out of his view. Hunching forward over the wheel, he jammed the accelerator to the floor and leaped left, tearing around the Buick and the bikers. The van threw water several feet into the air as he flew by.

As soon as he passed, he whipped the van back into the right lane. In the rear-view mirror he saw one of the bicycles hit the berm and its rider go flying off into the ditch. An instant later the other kid crashed off the road right behind him.

He shrugged when he saw the Buick leave the highway and pull in behind the kids.

Good for you, jerk. You and the little creeps can all get drenched together.

He could see her again, about three-quarters of a mile ahead. She went past the turnoff to the dam, her speed holding steady. Then her right turn signal came on, and she pulled off the highway.

Resisting the impulse to speed ahead and turn off behind her, he stayed on the road, slowing imperceptibly as he passed the dirt road she had taken.

The marker said Tridale Lane. Beneath it, on the same pole, a square brown-and-white sign read Leigh-Hi Farm.

Catchside pulled his black cap down an inch lower over his forehead and kept going.

TWELVE

All the way out to the farm, Freddi's emotions vacillated between simmering irritation and a swelling sense of dread.

The irritation was targeted at Mitch. When she had told him of her intention to spend the evening alone at the farm, he had begun to rail at her about her obstinacy.

"You're just as hardheaded as you ever were," he declared. "I'd think that after what happened to Jennifer this afternoon, you'd use a little better judgment."

He hadn't even had the courtesy to wait until they were outside. Instead he had started his harangue in front of the still-shaken Jennifer, while Daniel and Abby listened with obvious embarrassment.

At that point, Freddi had said a hurried good-bye to the others and pushed past him, right on out the door.

But Mitch wouldn't let it go. "There's nothing out there that won't wait until I can go with you," he insisted.

"I don't *need* you to go with me, Mitch."

The initial rush of pleasure Freddi had felt at his concern quickly gave way to annoyance at his overbearing attitude. "I'll be back at Abby's by eight, eight-thirty at the latest," she told him, striving to keep her voice level.

This attempt to placate him didn't work. He ended his tirade with the caustic observation that sometimes she didn't show "a lick of sense."

If she hadn't been so exasperated with him, Freddi now thought, it might have been almost amusing. She had managed to curb her own temper, waiting until he quieted, then sweetly requested the fax report he had brought with him from the campus. Mitch's parting shot as he smacked the report sharply into her hand had been something about her possessing "all the smarts of a grapefruit."

Oddly enough, the confrontation seemed to have melted at least one of the many walls of ice between them. Perhaps, Freddi thought with a smile, because it had brought things back to a more normal state of affairs. Conflict was familiar territory for her and Mitch.

The growing knot of dread in her midsection was due not to her argument with Mitch, however, but to the Monster

Man who continued to haunt her thoughts. Her talk with Henderson hadn't helped.

The detective, whose mood swings ranged from cynical to glum depending on what he had eaten, had been predictably morose throughout their telephone conversation that morning. Before hanging up, Henderson had warned her that anyone fitting the description of Freddi's stranger would assuredly fall into one of three categories: sociopath, psychopath, or lunatic.

"I'd opt for *lunatic,* seeing as how he has nothing more to do than slink around the woods in the rain," the detective had offered, just before promising a quick report.

Freddi's mind had been working overtime ever since learning of Abby's recurring dream early that morning. Her writer's imagination insisted on outlining a number of possible scenarios, all of them chilling.

Someone was stalking Abby, she was almost sure of it. And she was equally certain that the same person had been watching Abby's cabin — and Mitch's. In fact, Freddi had begun to sense that Mitch, and possibly anyone else associated with Abby, might be in danger.

The question was *why?* Why would

anyone want to hurt someone as innocent, as obviously harmless, as Abby?

And what about Abby's dream? Abby's *nightmare.*

Freddi shuddered as she recalled how Abby had wept and clung to her while describing the "dark water . . . and blood . . . and a man with a gun and no eyes." What could have happened in that poor confused woman's past to spawn such images of horror?

Questions. So many questions, and not an answer among them. With a sigh, Freddi reached to turn up the fan on the car's heater.

Approaching the turnoff to the farm, she shot a cursory glance in the rearview mirror and saw the dark van in the distance behind her.

Her gaze fixed on the mirror, she pulled off the highway onto the narrow dirt road that led to the farm and deliberately slowed the Mercedes to a crawl. The van passed the turnoff and went on up the highway without so much as slowing down.

Freddi sighed with relief and grinned sheepishly at her white-faced reflection in the mirror. There were probably only a hundred or more black vans in the county.

With a shake of her head, she started watching for the familiar blue-and-white buildings that checkered the right side of Tridale Lane, buildings that made up Leigh-Hi Farm.

Home. It was a heartening sight, if only for the sense of stability and permanence it offered.

For the first half hour inside the house, Freddi simply wandered through the rooms, looking, touching, remembering. Even though she had spent several hours here on her first day back, the same bitter-sweet waves of memory had rolled over her full force again tonight, almost as soon as she stepped out of the car.

In her old room, she now sat in the middle of the bed, her legs tucked snugly beneath her. Strange how the brick-walled room still seemed to hold the same cozy warmth that had blanketed her with security throughout all her growing-up years. The cherry four-poster was covered with the same Kentucky Rose quilt her grandmother had made before Freddi had even been born. Both front windows were still covered with the prim Cape Cods — obviously freshly laundered by Mrs. Kraker. Even the toddler-sized carousel horse carved for her by her great-uncle Robert stood in its usual place by the door, wearing its blue saddle and gold harness.

Freddi had been unprepared for her reaction to the house — in particular to this room, which had served as playroom, bedroom, and retreat. Here she had grown from girl to woman, and the walls still seemed to echo with her carefree, childish pranks, her girlhood dreams, her tears, her laughter, and her longings.

A sudden weariness washed over her. Could she really live here alone in this rambling old barn of a house, beloved as it was to her? Or was she merely deceiving herself, acting out a fantasy she had entertained for months? Should she have come back at all?

And Mitch. How did he really feel about her being here? Until that awful first meeting, it hadn't occurred to Freddi that he might resent her coming back. She had hoped for at least a hint of welcome, even while she had feared his indifference. What she hadn't anticipated was his barely concealed hostility.

She had thought she would be able to deal with his apathy, but the resentment, the bitterness behind his carefully impassive gaze, was breaking her heart.

And yet there had been moments when she thought she had glimpsed something else, some fleeting, elusive hint of a remembered smile in his eyes, a glint of fondness. Or had she only imagined it because she longed so desperately for some small sign of affection?

More questions with no answers. Freddi drew a long breath, then uncoiled her legs and swung her feet over the side of the bed. The only thing she could be reasonably certain of at present was the condition of the river. Before driving back into town tonight, she planned to make a run by the lower bank that edged almost the entire north side of the farm. She already knew what she would find: the river had to be close to overflowing its banks.

Freddi figured they had had at least four or five inches of rain by now. If it didn't stop soon, the Derry would surely reach crest by tomorrow. The dam worried her even more. Twice it had given way, and despite reinforcements and governmental assurances to the contrary, her grandfather had maintained that it would go again unless someone found a way to rechannel some of the spring floodwaters into separate tributaries.

Like most natives of the area, Freddi had

lived around the river too long to get panicky every time they had a hard rain. But this was more than a hard rain, and she felt increasingly uneasy about what it might do to the dam.

So why was she sitting here doing nothing?

Pushing herself off the bed, she went downstairs and started to work. After nearly an hour of searching through cabinets and cupboards, she had several stacks of photograph albums, scrapbooks, boxes of her grandmother's needlework, and other keepsakes heaped up in the middle of the hall, ready to be carried upstairs.

With a hefty load of items in her arms, she went up the stairway and started down the hall. There were four bedrooms on the second floor, one of which had never been used for anything other than storage. It was this room she planned to use now.

The door was open, but the room was dark. With her elbow, Freddi flipped the light switch and stepped inside, making a face at the damp, musty smell that greeted her.

The room was unfurnished except for an old daybed, her grandmother's treadle sewing machine, and some boxes. Freddi unloaded the albums on top of the daybed, pushing them flush to the wall so they wouldn't topple over. Then, leaving the light on, she went back downstairs for more.

She was almost to the top of the steps on her second trip when the lights went out, plunging the house into total darkness.

Stunned, Freddi teetered on the step, reeling from the sudden loss of vision and the burden in her arms. She felt a split second of panic. She leaned against the banister, then carefully shifted the box of needlework and scrapbooks from her arms to the top step. Slowly she started back downstairs, running one hand along the wall, gripping the banister with the other.

It was probably the storm. The wind was up and had been rattling the windowpanes for the last hour. Power outages were common throughout the county, especially during heavy rainstorms. Then, too, the house hadn't been occupied for over two years; there was no telling what condition the wiring might be in.

She stood unmoving at the bottom of the steps for another moment before turning and starting for the kitchen in search of a flashlight.

Just then a strong gust of wind hurled a wall of rain against the house. Her heart lunged, and she tripped, almost falling. She leaned against the wall for a moment to steady herself.

The roar of the wind and slashing rain made it difficult, nearly impossible, to hear. But Freddi heard *something* and held her breath, trying to identify the sound.

There. She froze, listening. From the back of the house — the kitchen — she heard it again. Louder this time. A rattling, then a thud.

Scarcely breathing, Freddi put her hand to the swinging door that opened into the kitchen, waiting.

Someone was trying to force the back door.

Her stomach knotted, and her pulse went crazy. *Wait,* she cautioned herself. *Just . . . wait.*

She dropped her hand away from the door, clenching and unclenching it at her side as she tried to draw a deep breath. A sudden howl of wind seized the house. Freddi jumped, then put her ear to the door, trying to hear what was happening on the other side.

Both the front and back doors were steel, equipped with deadbolts and security chains. The back door had even been braced with a chair shoved under the knob — Mrs. Kraker's doing, Freddi felt sure.

She knew for a fact that the doors and windows were all locked; she had checked them earlier when she first arrived at the house.

She held her breath and listened for a few more seconds but heard nothing. She was letting her imagination run wild, she told herself. This wasn't like her, to be so skittish. It was the storm, the worry about the dam, the black-clad stranger. If she wasn't careful, she was going to start acting like one of the characters in her own books.

The doors were a veritable fortress. Her grandfather had replaced them before Freddi had ever left home. No one was going to fool around with a steel door and a deadbolt.

Disgusted with herself, she expelled a sharp breath, then pushed the swinging door open, inch by inch. She stepped into the kitchen and stood, waiting.

She could see nothing. The room was black and silent. Freddi crept across the floor, feeling her way past the refrigerator, the electric range, then on to the sink. She fumbled for the drawers beside the sink and opening the second one on the right, blindly searched its contents. Nothing but silverware. She tried the one beside it, tugging at it a couple of times before the swollen wood finally let go with a screech.

She jumped, then froze for a moment before rummaging through numerous unidentifiable items. She caught a breath of relief when she found a box of safety matches. Not as good as a flashlight, but better than nothing.

She tried one more drawer. Almost as soon as she opened it, her hand closed over a full-size flashlight.

The batteries were still good. Aiming the beam of light at the floor and shading it with her other hand, Freddi started across the room, hovering close to the wall until she neared the window. She killed the flashlight, nudged the curtain slightly to one side, and looked out.

Nothing. Nothing but rain and darkness.

With the flashlight still out, she moved to the door to listen.

Again, nothing. Not a sound.

Obviously, she had heard only the wind. That had been her noise.

Then why was her heart still banging away at her rib cage?

She turned the flashlight on just long enough to glance at the face of her watch. When she saw it was almost nine-thirty, her stomach lurched. She had told Mitch she would be home by eight-thirty at the latest.

Not that Mitch was likely to worry about her, but Abby and Jennifer might. Freddi doused the light. At the moment, all she wanted to do was get out of the house and back to Abby's cabin. She would deal with the rest of the things in the hall tomorrow; hopefully by then the power would be restored.

Did she really intend to go outside? There was no light out there, either. No yard light, no moon, no stars.

Freddi shook her head, newly annoyed at herself. She was *going,* and that was that. It was late, she was tired, and she still hadn't even glanced at Henderson's report. She would go back to Abby's, have a hot shower and a cup of cocoa, in that order, and then find out what Henderson had dug up for her.

She switched on the flashlight and started across the kitchen, snatching her purse from the end of the counter. The fax report was still there, in the side pocket. All she had to do now was grab her raincoat from the hall closet, and she'd be out of here.

Freddi was only inches away from the swinging door when she heard a muffled thud at the front of the house.

She tensed. The only sound in the room was her heart pounding in her chest.

Suddenly she heard a sharp popping sound, then silence.

The front door.

She caught a breath and held it as her mind groped to identify the sound she had heard.

A gun. A gun with a silencer.

Her blood froze and her heart leaped to her throat. She saw the circle of light from her flashlight break up and realized that her hand was trembling almost uncontrollably.

Panic clutched at her throat as the image of an immense, dark-clad figure standing on the rise across from the campus flashed into her mind, and raw terror ricocheted through her body.

He was in the house.

Freddi knew with chilling certainty that she had only seconds to react. Her mind scrambled for focus.

He thinks I'm upstairs.

If he had been watching the house — and she knew with a sudden sick clarity that he had — he would have seen the light go on in the spare bedroom shortly before the power blew.

He'll head upstairs. . . . I have time. . . .

Suddenly, a firestorm exploded in Freddi's stomach. The ulcer that had been dormant for nearly a month roared to life. Clammy perspiration beaded her forehead as she gripped the flashlight. With her free hand, she clutched her purse to her stomach, bending nearly double at the unexpected surge of pain.

She couldn't afford to wait until the attack subsided. Keeping the flashlight beam low, she turned and retraced her steps across the kitchen. At the back door, she carefully pried the chair free, then held the flashlight with one hand as she fumbled to release the security chain and the deadbolt with the other.

Outside, Freddi practically hurled herself off the back porch and around the side of the house. Mindless of the rain slashing her face and body, she raced across the yard, wet mud sucking at her feet.

A hot flame of agony was burning in her stomach, but she tried to ignore it. The pain surged, but she didn't falter, slowing her speed only when she rounded the corner at the front of the house.

One glance at the front door standing open confirmed her fear: He was inside. It wouldn't take him long to realize that she *wasn't.*

With the beam of the flashlight trained on the ground just ahead of her, Freddi ran for the gravel driveway and the Mercedes, digging her keys out of her purse as she went.

She hit the electronic door opener, her eyes scanning the car, locking on the tires.

The front tires were flat! Shredded almost savagely.

Stunned, Freddi leaned against the car. Raw panic hit her full force now, threatening to overtake her reason. The pain in her stomach and the mounting horror of her situation brought hot tears to her eyes.

She swiveled, staring at the house, the gaping front door.

She couldn't give in to the fear. . . . That's exactly what he would expect . . . what he wanted.

She tried to pray. *Lord, you are "my stronghold and my deliverer, my shield, in whom I take refuge. . . ."*

Forcing a deep, steadying breath, Freddi hesitated for only an instant. Then she pushed away from the car, broke into the open, and bolted across the field toward the road.

Fear urged her on as she raced across the road into a wedge of overgrown pasture-land that led to the river. She had to avoid the highway. She would be completely at his mercy if he came after her in the van. Her best chance was to hide in the belt of woods that rimmed the river. She knew them nearly as well as she knew the inside of the house. There, she would have the advantage and just might be able to lose him.

Freddi stopped for only an instant to let her eyes scan the gentle swell of ground that formed a natural ridge above the riverbank. The slope down to the river was thick with underbrush and dense with berry thickets and briers, but she had no choice.

Her back to the road, she strained to see any trace of a clearing. Suddenly, the roar of an engine exploded out of the night, and a blaze of light pinned her in its glare.

Freddi's mind swung out of control. She whipped around, away from the lights, and poised at the top of the bank, ready to leap down the slope.

A car door slammed. Freddi panicked and lost her footing on the mud-slickened incline. Her hands shot out, flailing wildly in search of something to grab, finding nothing but wind and rain.

"Freddi!"

Arms went around her, yanked her backward, and held her as she screamed into the night.

THIRTEEN

On a dead run, Mitch pulled Freddi across the field to the truck, trying to shelter her beneath his raincoat. "It's OK; it's OK," he kept saying as they ran. He had left the Ranger idling. Quickly he helped her into the seat, but when he would have closed the door, she continued to clutch his arm. Her eyes were wild, glazed with a terror that made Mitch's own heart race. He waited, holding her, letting her hold him.

"What happened?" When she didn't answer, he prompted, "Freddi? Are you hurt?"

Freddi stared at him blankly for a moment, then shook her head. "He was in the house. . . . He broke into the house. . . ."

Mitch heard the rising note of hysteria in her voice. "Who, Freddi? *Who* was in the house?"

Her skin was deathly pale. Lunging forward, she tightened her hands on his arm. "We have to get out of here!"

She turned toward the house. *"Mitch! Look!"*

Mitch saw a flash of light distorted by the rain.

Headlights. A car was pulling away from the house.

"*Mitch!*" Freddi screamed, pushing at him. "Hurry!"

Mitch locked her door, then bolted to the driver's side of the Ranger and, throwing himself behind the wheel, slammed the truck into gear.

"Your seat belt," he snapped at Freddi as he whipped the truck around. Flooring the accelerator, he took off toward the main highway.

At the intersection he braked hard, then veered left. He roared down the road toward town, tugging his seat belt over his shoulder and securing it as he went.

With one eye on the rearview mirror, Mitch pushed the pickup as hard as he dared in the storm. Chunks of mud blotted the road, runoff from the mountain slopes bordering the highway. Wind-driven rain and fog engulfed the truck, and he couldn't see more than a few feet ahead.

He glanced over at Freddi. She was still shaking, but she didn't look quite as terrified now.

"Freddi? You all right?"

Freddi didn't answer but instead struggled against the confines of the seat belt as she tried to look out the back window. Automatically, Mitch glanced into the rear-view mirror again.

Nothing but dark road behind them.

With his eyes on the highway, he reached for Freddi's hand. "Hey, kiddo, can you talk to me? What happened?"

Slowly, she dragged her gaze away from the rear window and fixed her eyes on him. Finally she nodded, her expression clearing.

"It was him," she said in a choked voice. "Jennifer followed him this afternoon. He . . . broke into the house. He shot the lock off the front door."

Mitch twisted to look at her.

"He thought I was trapped upstairs."

He squeezed her hand. "Where were you?"

"Downstairs. In the kitchen. The storm had knocked the power out a few minutes before and —"

Freddi stopped, her gaze sweeping the road, first one side, then the other.

The highway lights were on.

"The power's not out, Freddi," Mitch pointed out needlessly.

Her hand gripped his. "I think I knew that." Turning in the seat, she clutched his arm. "He'll come after us, Mitch. We have to —"

Mitch saw the wavering glow of head-lights in the rearview mirror before she did. Expelling a sharp breath, he withdrew his hand from hers and gripped the steering wheel. His eyes darted back and forth from the mirror to the road as he drove.

Freddi looked at him, then twisted to look out the back window. *"Mitch!"*

"Don't worry," he said shortly. "I'll lose him." *Please, Lord.*

The headlights were moving up fast. Too fast. Mitch pushed the accelerator almost to the floor.

"What are we going to do?"

Mitch heard the panic in her voice, and it shook him. It took a lot to rattle Freddi. Just knowing she was scared sharpened his own fear.

The headlights were gaining when he saw the sign for Perkins Road just ahead on the right and knew what he was going to do.

Toward the crest of the hill an S-curve bent right, then sharply left again. He cut his speed so he wouldn't lose control.

"Mitch —"

"It's OK," he mumbled, almost on top of the turnoff now. He switched off his lights, shrouding the truck in the darkness and pounding rain.

"Mitch, what are you *doing?*"

"Taking the scenic route," he said shortly. "Hang on."

He snapped the truck right, hard, shooting off the highway onto Perkins Road.

With his lights off, he bounced down the narrow, pitted road, praying there were no new killer chuckholes since he'd driven down it last week.

"You can't see!" Freddi cried, her voice pitched high with alarm.

"And neither can *he.*"

He felt her watching him.

Finally, he slowed the Ranger almost to a stop, keeping his eyes on the rearview mirror.

Seconds passed. Then, just as Mitch had hoped, the van roared by, tearing on down the highway. The hunter in search of his prey.

He looked over at Freddi, unable to see her face in the darkness. "Still all right?"

He heard her catch her breath. "Sure." Her voice held a tremor, but she sounded more like herself. "I haven't had a ride like that since the last time I was in a pickup with you."

"Missed it, have you?"

She was silent for an instant. "Are you going to take this cow path all the way into town?"

"That's the idea. Unless you'd rather play tag with your friend in the van."

There was a pause. "Can we at least have headlights the rest of the way?"

"If it'll make you feel better."

"The only thing that would make me feel better right now is an armed escort."

"City life has made you soft, girl."

After another moment, Mitch started down the road, switching on the Ranger's parking lights for the first hundred yards or so before adding the headlights.

When he was sure they were safe, he couldn't resist reminding her of her foolishness. "I *told* you not to come out here alone," he said, staring straight ahead at the narrow road, eerily distorted in the rain-sheeted haze of the headlights.

He could almost hear her teeth grinding. "If it will make you feel better to say, 'I told you so,' Mitch, then by all means, go ahead."

He didn't answer. She didn't need to know that he had been terrified out of his mind all the way out to the farm, thinking something had happened to her. Something terrible.

She was silent for another moment. "What exactly are you doing out here, anyway?" Her voice was testy.

Mitch felt his face heat with irritation. "I'd say that's fairly obvious. I was trying to save your neck."

"Oh, *really*," she drawled, her tone dripping acid.

Mitch's hands tightened on the wheel. He didn't think he'd ever forget the sight of her standing out there on the rise of the riverbank, soaked to her skin, looking for all the world like a cornered bobcat.

Still he refused to let her bait him. "You said you'd be back by eight-thirty at the latest. I was afraid — you might have had car trouble." He couldn't fight with her. Not now. He was still paralyzed inside by the thought of what could have happened to her if she hadn't made it out of that house. . . .

"What are we going to do?" The sharp edge in her voice made him flinch.

"First, we're going to go to the police." A thought struck him. "What was in that fax report?"

Freddi looked at him blankly. "I haven't even opened it yet. I was going to read it after I got back to Abby's."

He switched on the truck's interior light.

"Maybe you'd better check it before we get into town."

She pulled the envelope from her purse and ripped it open. "You're not going to go to Bannon, are you?" she asked, scanning the first page.

Mitch shook his head. "No, there's a new fellow on the force who seems pretty savvy. Tom Robbins. I've talked with him a few times, and I like him. Maybe he can help." He paused, watching her as she read. "Anything?"

She didn't respond right away. Her eyes widened as she read until, abruptly, she turned to him. "Mitch — is Abby alone? Is she still at the cabin?"

Mitch looked at her, then shook his head. "No. I took her down to my place before I left. She's with Dan and Jennifer. Why?"

Freddi nodded shortly, turning her attention back to the report. After another moment, she caught a sharp breath.

"Freddi, will you tell me —"

Her head still bent over the report, she waved away his interruption. "In a minute."

Mitch shot a look into the rearview mirror, sinking back against the seat a little when he saw that the road was still dark behind them.

Finally, Freddi looked up. She kept her face set straight ahead for a long moment. Then she turned to him. "Mitch, we can talk with this — Robbins — if you want, but I think we ought to call the state police first."

He swung around to look at her, and she lifted the report in a gesture of explanation. "Henderson was able to ID the photo I faxed him."

Mitch nodded, waiting.

"The guy's name is Catchside. Floyd Catchside." She paused, then added, "Among other things, he's most likely a contract killer."

Mitch shot her a startled look.

"I told you I sent a photo of Abby, too —"

Again he nodded.

Freddi expelled a long breath. "If Henderson's right," she said tightly, "Abby's the bottom line on an old contract."

He held his breath.

"He's here to kill her, Mitch."

FOURTEEN

Abby hadn't meant to eavesdrop on the conversation. It was just that it had been impossible *not* to listen, once she had heard what they were talking about.

Something was wrong, terribly wrong. Mitch and Freddi hadn't come back to the cabin until very late — almost eleven. And when they *did* finally return they were both so — peculiar. Why, Freddi had been positively *drenched* — and so nervous. And Mitch — she had never seen him in such a state, pacing the floor, jingling his keys, snapping at poor little Pork Chop. He wasn't a bit like himself, not at all.

And the way he'd insisted that they all stay together, here in his cabin, for the rest of the night — as if he were frightened about something.

Abby knew that he and Freddi had gone to the police. That was one of the reasons they were so late, Mitch had explained, rather vaguely. They had gone to see a policeman named Robbins, as well as the state police. Abby was sure there was something else, something he wasn't telling, but of course she didn't ask.

Finally, thinking she might be in the way — young people needed time alone, after all — Abby had said good night and come up to the bedroom. *Mitch's* bedroom, where, according to his instructions, she and Freddi were to spend the night. He would take the couch in the living room.

Only a moment ago, however, Abby had decided to go back downstairs and get Pork Chop. The little cocker had been tagging after her all evening in Mitch's absence, and his antics *did* help take her mind off Peaches.

She had started to open the bedroom door, then stopped, her attention caught by Freddi's voice. . . .

"The widow of *Roger* Chase," Freddi said, dropping down onto a plump quilted pillow in front of the fireplace. "You know — the health resort developer. He and his granddaughter, Melissa, were murdered a few years ago, on his yacht in Virginia, the *Lady A.* The case was never closed." She paused. "Abigail Chase was the main suspect."

Jennifer set a tray of mugs of steaming coffee on the table in front of the couch. Straightening, she turned to look at Freddi.

"*Abigail* Chase?" she repeated softly.

Freddi nodded, tugging at the legs of the warm-up suit Jennifer had lent her. "Abigail was Roger's second wife. His first wife died of a heart attack in the late seventies."

Daniel leaned over to rub Sunny's ears. "You said Abigail Chase was the primary suspect. Why?"

"Because she was the surviving heir after Melissa — Roger's granddaughter. Abigail was on the yacht the day of the murders, too, but she escaped unharmed." Freddi reached for the mug of coffee Jennifer handed her and set it on the hearth. "Apparently Chase's only child — Melissa's mother — OD'd on heroine and died when Melissa was still a baby. Roger Chase raised his granddaughter, and he adored the girl. The way his will was set up, if anything were to happen to Melissa, then his wife, Abigail, stood to inherit the entire estate — and apparently it's a *considerable* estate."

Mitch had been standing at the sliding-glass doors, his back turned as he stared out into the night. He turned now and came over to the table, smiling his thanks to Jennifer as he lifted a cup of coffee from the tray.

Mitch looked weary, Jennifer thought as

she scooted in beside Daniel on the couch and guided his hand to a cup of coffee. Weary and *worried.*

"Was Abigail Chase ever brought to trial?" Daniel asked.

"No," replied Freddi. "There was a hearing, but shortly after it started, Abigail's mind apparently just — snapped. The court dismissed the hearing and placed her in a sanitarium for treatment. The estate was tied up from that point on with one legal maneuver after another. Taylor Chase, Roger's brother, tried everything to break the will — he was next in line to inherit after Abigail — but he never got anywhere."

Daniel stopped Freddi before she could go on. "You said Abigail's mind snapped — ?"

Freddi began to shuffle pages. "Yes . . . wait, it's further on. Here. According to the newspaper accounts, early in the hearing Abigail became — these are Henderson's words — 'extremely agitated, incoherent, and irrational.' It seems that she kept raving about a white-haired stranger." Freddi paused. "A white-haired stranger with no eyes."

"No *eyes?*" Jennifer shuddered at the description. Beside her, Daniel touched her arm as if he sensed her uneasiness.

Nodding, Freddi elaborated. "When they took her out of the courtroom for the last time, Abigail was screaming something about her husband and Melissa being murdered by a man with white hair and no eyes. That's all she could remember."

Jennifer put a hand to her throat. *White hair . . . the stranger in the woods had white hair . . . and dark glasses. . . .*

Freddi's voice was laced with disgust. "His name is Floyd Catchside. He's thought to be a hired assassin — very professional, very ruthless, and *very* weird. Unfortunately, he seems to be as elusive as he is dangerous. He was court-martialed for some kind of trouble in Vietnam but got out of it. Henderson said he bounced around Central America for a couple of years as a mercenary. Off and on he's done some drug running. You name it. If it's illegal, Catchside has done it." Her eyes darkened. "But his specialty," she said grimly, "seems to be murder — contract killings. And from what Henderson has been able to learn, he thoroughly enjoys his work. He's also smart. *Very* smart."

"Sounds like a real creep." Mitch's voice was as hard as his eyes.

"The worst kind," Freddi agreed. "Incidentally, Catchside is an albino. White hair, pale eyes. He has some vision problems — and several allergies. For reasons of his own," she said, glancing up from the report, "he always wears black."

A net of tension stretched over the room, and Jennifer suddenly felt extremely cold. "Then he's the one Abigail Chase was talking about — the one who killed her family."

Freddi dropped the report into her lap, nodding. "He's also the man in Abby's nightmare," she said. Wiping a hand across her eyes in a gesture of fatigue, she described Abby's dream in detail.

"Freddi —" Daniel leaned forward on the couch, his elbows braced on his knees. "Is there any doubt whatsoever that Abby *is* Abigail Chase?"

"None, Daniel. Henderson made a positive ID from the photo I sent. You'd have to know him. Henderson probably has a complete mental file on every unsolved murder in the country over the past twenty years. The guy's a walking database." She took a deep breath, then let it out. "Anyway, he said Abigail Chase walked away from a sanitarium in Virginia early last fall and just — disappeared. There was a search, of course, but she was never found."

"That would have been about the time that Abby showed up here," Mitch put in.

Daniel leaned back and crossed his arms over his chest. "So . . . if Abby is really Abigail Chase, and if Catchside is the one who killed her family, then there isn't any question as to why he's here, is there?"

"That's right," Freddi said quickly. "As long as she's alive, there's always the chance she might recover —"

"And cause a whole lot of trouble for whoever murdered her family — or whoever had it *done*," Daniel finished for her. "Any ideas on who that might be?"

"Roger's brother," Freddi answered without the slightest hesitation. "Taylor Chase. Henderson checked on the will. Taylor is next in line to inherit the estate if both Roger's granddaughter and Abigail are deceased. But," she pointed out with a meaningful look, "the fact that Abigail is missing doesn't constitute a legal death. The estate could be tied up for years unless Taylor can prove that she's dead."

"I don't understand how she managed to get off that yacht alive," Jennifer said.

"She went overboard," said Freddi. "The Coast Guard picked her up a couple of hours later. Apparently her husband must have lived long enough to get off a May-day. Anyway, Abigail was critically ill with pneumonia for weeks afterward; that's one of the reasons the hearing was delayed."

"And there was no sign of this . . . Catchside . . . when they rescued her?" Daniel asked.

"None. It was as if he didn't exist. That's why no one would believe Abigail's story. I figure he probably had a boat waiting for him — someone dropped him off and picked him up."

"How do you suppose Abby made her way *here* from Virginia? And why has it taken so long for this — Catchside — to find her?" Jennifer asked.

"Sometimes it's the people who aren't really *trying* to disappear who actually are the most successful," Freddi replied. "Their movements are so completely un-planned that it's next to impossible to trace them. A real pro can almost always track down a person who's predictable, but Abby probably just walked off the grounds and kept right on moving. No logic, no destination, no predictable pattern."

"Psychogenic fugue," Daniel said thoughtfully.

Freddi looked at him. "That has some-thing to do with amnesia, doesn't it?"

Daniel nodded. "People suffering from

certain kinds of amnesia sometimes just — disappear. They wander off, start new lives — nobody really knows what motivates them. In Abby's case, even though she can't remember events prior to the trauma that brought on the amnesia, she probably has some degree of residual memory, a type of subconscious record of what happened to her. She may have wandered away from the sanitarium because she was unknowingly looking for something — or some*one*."

"We *do* know she came here on a bus," Mitch offered. "She had been in Ashland and Huntington — she remembered the names of those two cities but nothing much before that."

"There's something I don't understand," Jennifer said abruptly. "If *Abby* is the reason for this — Catchside — being here, then why did he show up at Freddi's farm tonight? Why did he terrorize *Freddi* when Abby's the one he's after?"

There was a long silence before Freddi answered quietly. "I'm afraid we're all targets now, Jennifer. Catchside is like a search-and-destroy weapon. Abigail Chase is his target, and he's going to go straight for her, eliminating anything or anyone that gets in his way. For all Catchside knows, Abby may have remembered what happened that day on the yacht and confided it to one — or all — of us." She stopped, then added, "We're probably in as much danger as Abby is, just because we're a part of her life."

"Mitch in particular," Daniel said quietly.

"That's right," Freddi agreed heavily. "Mitch in particular."

"What can we do?" Jennifer asked, instinctively moving a little closer to Daniel.

"The state police are going to give us as much help as they can," Mitch replied. "They've already put out an APB on Catchside. And Tom Robbins — he's new on the city police force — jumped right in, too. He promised to make extra runs by both cabins and patrol the Ridge as closely as possible. Meanwhile —" He paused, making eye contact with each of them for a moment before going on. "We all stay together. Freddi had a close call tonight. I think we'll find more safety in numbers."

Abby stepped back inside the bedroom, closing the door as quietly as possible.

The room seemed to sway around her. Her vision blurred, and she reached for the edge of the bureau, clutching at it with a trembling hand. Her blood surged; bile rose in her throat, and she pressed a hand to her mouth. Her mind went racing backward, tumbling out of control down a dark, slippery corridor to the past. . . .

Roger . . . and Missa . . .

Dead. Both of them, dead . . . on the yacht.

She had been below deck, starting up the stairs when she heard Missa's panicky screams. She began to run. . . .

She had seen Roger first, struggling with an enormous man in black clothing, a giant of a man wearing dark glasses . . . and holding a gun.

Her own screams had drowned out Missa's. The big man's head swung around, long enough for Roger to force the hand with the gun backward. The man staggered, then righted himself, aimed the gun at Roger.

Missa threw herself in front of her grandfather. . . . There were shots. . . . Missa fell first, then Roger.

"Get off the boat," he cried out as he fell. *"Jump, Abby! Jump!"*

The man turned toward Abby, and she flew at him, screaming, pounding at him. He was like a wall of granite. She clawed at his eyes, knocked the dark glasses from him as she raked her nails across his face. He threw a hand over his eyes to shield them, then lowered the same hand to strike her.

But his eyes . . . they were like nothing Abby had ever seen. Nightmare eyes, with a monstrous, unknown evil staring out at her from some vast, cold chamber.

She saw Roger move. He was still alive! She made the decision to go overboard, to lure the mad giant away from Roger and Missa, to give them a chance. . . .

The man hesitated a moment before diving in after her. The water was cold, so cold and dark. Abby went underneath the yacht as he circled above her. She moved, grabbing air whenever she could. He seemed awkward in the water, clumsy and disoriented.

Using what little strength she had left, Abby began to swim out, away from the *Lady A*, staying below the water as much as possible, putting distance between them.

But he came after her — awkwardly at first, but then closer . . . closer. Her arms were lead, her legs had weights on them, the water sucked her down. Her ears were pounding, her heart hammering. She fought to go on, pushed her head above water.

There was a noise, a loud churning, like the sound of an engine.

Then nothing . . . nothing but dark water.

Abby opened her mouth to scream, but the only sound that came out was a soft cry of despair. Slowly, blankly, she looked around the room.

The dark water was gone. But Catchside was back.

This wasn't the first time she had remembered fragments, pieces of a horror she wanted only to forget. Sometimes in the middle of the day while she was working in the cafeteria or cleaning for Mitch, a puzzle would form in her mind and something would try to nudge a piece into place, close enough that she could almost feel her memory touching it. But then it would slip away, disappearing before she could fit it back where it belonged.

Now the pieces were all coming together at once, and it was too much, too fast.

Abby began to cry. She cried as she had never cried before. Tears boiled up in her throat, spilled from her eyes, poured down her face. Tears for the family she had loved and lost, for the time that had been torn away from her. Tears of remembered grief — and renewed dread.

FIFTEEN

"Daniel, is Abby going to be all right?" Jennifer whispered in the darkness of the bedroom.

Still dressed, Daniel sat on the side of the bed, absently stroking Sunny's head. "I think so. She'll probably need some professional help for a while, but once she comes through the shock of getting her memory back, I believe she'll handle everything else all right."

Jennifer propped herself up on her pillow, studying his shadowed profile. He rubbed a hand down one side of his face in a gesture of fatigue, and she reached to touch his arm. "Shouldn't you try to get some sleep? It's almost two."

Shaking his head, he stretched his arms out in front of him, then dropped his hands to his knees. "I just came in to see about you. I've been worried about you all day, after what happened on the hill. Do you think you can sleep now?"

"My scare was nothing compared to Freddi's. I'm all right."

"Then I think I'll go sit with Mitch. He's

wired pretty tight."

No one was getting any sleep tonight, Jennifer thought wearily. Just after midnight she and Freddi had decided to turn in. Upstairs, however, they had found Abby crying her heart out, on the verge of hysteria.

From then on the focus of everyone's attention had been Abby. Daniel had been so good with her. At one point, everyone had been trying a little *too* hard to help the distraught woman, and she had seemed to become even more distressed. Daniel had finally stepped in, suggesting that perhaps he could help if Abby wouldn't mind speaking alone with him.

He had stayed with her for well over an hour, and finally Abby had drifted off to sleep.

Which was more than any of the rest of them had managed to do. Jennifer sat up in bed, hugging her knees to her chest. "I can't even begin to imagine what it must be like for Abby," she said. "Not only did she have to endure the horror of seeing her family murdered once, but now it's almost as if she's reliving it *again*." Her heart ached for the small, sweet-natured woman who had so quickly endeared herself to all of them.

"That's probably more accurate than you think," Daniel said. "My impression was that her memories are almost as ugly and as terrifying as what she witnessed firsthand."

Jennifer rested her head on her propped-up knees. "No wonder her mind blocked it out for so long. Maybe it was the only way she was able to survive the whole ordeal."

"I'm not so sure it was altogether the trauma of the murders that triggered Abby's amnesia," Daniel said, leaning back and bracing himself on one elbow. "I think her feelings of helplessness may have played a part in the memory loss. One of the things I sensed in her tonight was a certain amount of frustration. And possibly some guilt as well."

Jennifer looked at him. "*Guilt?* But why? There was nothing she could have done —"

"But she thinks she *should* have been able to do something," he pointed out, "and that's probably been gnawing at her all this time, even if she wasn't aware of it." He turned toward her. "Worse yet, she now believes she may have jeopardized someone else she loves — Mitch — and perhaps the rest of us."

"Poor Abby," Jennifer murmured. "Were

you able to help her?"

He was quiet for a moment. "I tried. But I understand her feelings, Jennifer. I've felt them all myself, at one time or another."

Jennifer touched his arm as he went on. "It's going to take more than words to give Abby any real peace. She needs to see an end to her nightmare. She needs to feel safe again and to know that Mitch is safe, too."

Jennifer sank back against the headboard. "There's no way Abby or Mitch — or any of the rest of us — can possibly feel safe until this . . . madman is stopped." She sighed. "How do we manage to get ourselves into these situations anyway, Daniel? It seems as though every time we leave home, we end up in trouble."

Daniel shrugged and attempted a weak smile. "I suppose it's just a case of being in the right place at the right time."

"I certainly don't see anything *right* about any of this," Jennifer muttered. "It seems like the wrong place at the wrong time."

"Don't be too sure," he said quietly. "The Lord has a way of putting us where he wants us, even if it isn't exactly where we'd like to be. Things may not look so great to us, or even make a lot of sense —

but that's because we can't see the entire picture. He can."

He reached for her, wrapping her snugly in his arms. When she burrowed her head gratefully into the warm strength of his shoulder, he pressed a gentle kiss against her hair.

"Don't worry," he said softly. "We're going to come out of this all right. You'll see."

Jennifer wished she shared his optimism. For that matter, she wondered if he was really as confident as he sounded.

After a moment, Daniel gently brushed his lips across her forehead, then eased her out of his arms and back onto the pillow. "I'll take Sunny out to the living room with me. You get some sleep now."

"You need to rest, too, Daniel —"

"I'll doze in the living room," he said, getting up from the bed and tucking the blanket around her shoulders.

As she sank down into the pillows, Jennifer realized that neither Daniel nor Mitch had any intention of going to sleep. To the contrary, they were going to stand guard.

The ringing of the telephone was distant but demanding. Squinting into the darkness of the bedroom, Jennifer waited out another three rings before sitting up.

A web of light from the pole lamp outside the cabin seeped into the room. Glancing at the clock on the nightstand, she saw that it was two forty-five; she had been asleep only a few minutes.

She thought she could hear Mitch talking in the kitchen. After another moment, she heard him go down the hall toward the living room and call upstairs. With a sigh Jennifer turned on the lamp, swung her feet over the side of the bed, and shrugged into her robe.

By the time she walked into the living room, Freddi, still dressed in Jennifer's red warm-up suit, was halfway down the stairs. Right behind her came Abby, also dressed but looking slightly dazed. Both Daniel and Mitch were standing in the middle of the room.

Freddi started firing questions at Mitch as soon as she cleared the steps. "It's the river, isn't it? Did it go over?"

He nodded grimly. "It's already up about two feet downtown, more in the south end."

Freddi twisted her mouth to one side. "I thought we had until afternoon anyway."

Mitch shook his head. "I've got to get down to the campus. They'll start bringing people in soon."

Freddi nodded, then turned to Jennifer. "The campus is the main shelter in a flood. It's high enough to be safe. There are only a couple of others — a church at the north end of town and the high school."

Jennifer felt the first stirring of fear. "Then there *is* going to be a flood?"

Freddi smiled thinly. "Welcome to springtime in Derry Ridge. But you don't have to worry about it up here, Jennifer. The town takes the worst of it."

Jennifer glanced at Abby and saw that her expression was pinched and frightened as she wrung her hands at her waist.

Apparently Mitch, too, had sensed Abby's agitation. He went to her and put a hand on her shoulder. "It's all right, Abby. Remember, I told you what it would be like in case of a flood. We'll be fine."

Abby looked up at him. "How high will the water get, Mitch?"

He shook his head. "There's no way of knowing. But it won't bother us up here." He turned to Freddi. "That was Tom Robbins who called. The police want everyone who can help to meet at the student center. Do you want to go with me?"

"We'll all go," said Daniel. "We can take the Cherokee."

Mitch looked at him, then met Jennifer's eyes over the top of Abby's head. "I . . . thought maybe the two of you could stay here with Abby," he said uncertainly.

Daniel frowned. After a moment, his expression cleared. "Whatever will help most," he said evenly.

Jennifer swallowed hard at the look of regret on her husband's face. Obviously the feelings of helplessness he had described to her earlier were stirring once again. It was only natural that he would want to go with Mitch, to help however he could. Instead, he was being asked to stay here with two women. Just as certainly, she knew that he would assume that Mitch had made the suggestion because of his blindness.

But Freddi's perception and acute sense of timing turned the situation around. Darting a sharp-eyed glance from Daniel to Mitch, she said bluntly, "I thought you said we should all stay together, Mitch. Besides, they're going to need all the help they can get at the campus, aren't they?"

Mitch opened his mouth to say something, but Abby didn't give him a chance. "Freddi is absolutely right, Mitch," she said, her voice unexpectedly firm. "Why, I can't just sit up here when there's so much to be done! My goodness, think of the food they're going to need. I should go right now."

Mitch frowned, obviously surprised by the strength of Abby's reaction. "But, Abby, you'll be safer right here," he insisted. "You won't have to worry about the flood up here —"

"I won't have to worry about the flood down *there*, either," she announced briskly, leveling her blue-eyed gaze at him. "I'll be much too busy. You young people can deal with the flood; I'll help take care of the food."

Jennifer looked at Daniel. Standing with his arms crossed comfortably over his chest, he was grinning openly.

"Abby, you and I *could* use some clothes," Freddi told her. "Why don't you let Daniel and Jennifer take you up to your place in their car and collect some things for both of us? While you're doing that, Mitch and I can go on down to the center in the truck. We can all meet there."

As if he were determined not to give anyone a chance to nix Freddi's suggestion, Daniel jumped in. "Sounds good, Freddi. We probably ought to have both vehicles down at the campus anyway. Abby, is that all right with you?"

Abby had already started for the stairs.

"I'll only be a minute, Daniel. Just let me get my purse."

Suddenly Jennifer realized that she was still in her bathrobe. She started for the bathroom. "I can't go *anywhere* until I get dressed."

"You're not going to do your hair, are you?" Daniel asked.

She stopped, turning to look at him. "What do you mean?"

He raised one eyebrow. "Just that we may not have forty days and forty nights for this one."

SIXTEEN

It took no more than fifteen minutes in the crowded student center for the dull stomach pain Freddi had been fighting most of the night to develop into a full-blown ulcer attack. Her stomach burned as the acids flared, undoubtedly aggravated by the news of the flood and all the commotion in the lobby.

Both she and Mitch had been put to work the instant they arrived. A Civil Defense volunteer stopped Mitch in the parking lot. Inside, someone thrust a clipboard and a pencil into Freddi's hands with vague instructions about the need for a list of the evacuees already on the premises, as well as those yet to come.

As she pencilled in her most recent entry, she stood near the entrance to the cafeteria, letting her gaze scan the scene in the lobby. The entire center was teeming with noise and confusion. With evacuation already in progress in several parts of town, dozens of families were milling about the building. Crying children tugged at the legs of worried-looking mothers, who were trying to follow the instructions of those in charge. Several tired-looking men with rain-slicked hair and dripping jackets paced the length of the lobby, snapping curt orders or clearing obstacles out of the way. A police officer threaded his way through the crowd, his radio crackling with static as he separated those who genuinely needed shelter from those who had come out of mere curiosity.

Students and faculty members from the college were hurriedly outfitting one entire wing of the lobby with sleeping bags and blankets. At the opposite end, aluminum tables and chairs had been arranged to serve as an information center for rescue workers and displaced family members.

Parting a huddle of teenagers in the middle of the room, Mitch approached. He was still in his rain slicker, his hair soaked. "Dan and Jennifer haven't shown up with Abby yet, have they?" he asked, his eyes roaming over the room.

Freddi tucked the clipboard under one arm and shook her head. "They'll probably be another half hour or more, I imagine, by the time Jennifer changes and they get up to Abby's."

"I hope Jennifer doesn't have any trouble driving down here," he said. Several spots along the road had been slick with mud on their way in, and twice Mitch had stopped to clear fallen tree limbs and other debris out of the way.

"Have you been outside all this time?" Freddi asked him.

"We were trying to get most of the cars off the parking lot," he answered, slipping out of his dripping raincoat, "in case we need the space later."

Static hissed nearby, and police officer Tom Robbins appeared. He shot Freddi a quick smile before turning to Mitch. "They tell me you're the man to see for some answers."

"Only if the questions are easy. What do you need?"

"I *need* about six more men and eight hours' sleep, but I'll settle for a little information. This is my first flood situation. Are we dealing with anything major here?"

Mitch paused, then nodded. "Anytime you've got a river the size of the Derry spilling over its banks — and a dam that's kept the whole county looking over its shoulder for more than twenty years — I suppose you need to think in terms of something major."

"I was hoping you'd tell me not to worry." Robbins raked a hand through his salt-and-pepper hair as his gaze surveyed the congested lobby. "Any estimate as to how many people may end up here over the next few hours?"

"That depends on how high and how fast the water rises," Mitch answered. "I can tell you this much: we have only three shelters, and they've never been enough. Last time we had to put tents up outside to handle everybody. We also ended up with a few who were injured and couldn't make it across town to the hospital."

Robbins looked at him with the hint of a grim smile. "I sure feel a lot better about things now that I've talked with you, Professor. Maybe I'll look you up again later." He lifted his hand in a parting wave as he answered a call on the radio and moved through the lobby.

Mitch watched Robbins walk away before turning back to Freddi. "Does that fall under the heading of creative writing?" He inclined his head toward the clipboard.

"It's as creative as I'm going to get for now. Do you suppose they have coffee made yet?"

"Should have. I'd rather wait for some of Abby's, but I'm cold and wet enough to drink just about anything hot. Let me get rid of this raincoat, and we'll see —"

The shriek of a police whistle pierced the din in the lobby and cut Mitch off midsentence. Tom Robbins yelled for quiet, then turned up the volume on a nearby portable radio. Within seconds, even the children had quieted enough that the radio announcer could be heard.

"This is a special bulletin for Derry Ridge and surrounding areas: Waters of the Derry River and Vision Lake are rising at the rate of almost a foot an hour. Both the Derry and Vision Lake are overflowing their banks. Worsening the problem is the fact that the Ryder Bridge collapsed only moments ago, jamming Vision Lake and causing the water to rise even faster.

"There are reports of smaller bridges out and roads closed throughout the county. Residents in several communities are being evacuated as quickly as possible. Anyone residing in a flood-watch district is advised to stay tuned for further bulletins and to be prepared for immediate evacuation if necessary.

"In response to the numerous inquiries this station has received regarding the condition of Derry Dam, please be advised that no updated information has been communicated to us by county officials. Attention has focused over recent months on the effectiveness of the existing

discharge system, as well as a rumored dishing of the dam at its middle, but to date we are aware of no revised reports on either of these conditions. . . ."

The rest of the announcer's statement was lost, overpowered by the sudden, repeated screaming of a siren. With a sharp clutch of fear, Freddi recognized the sound of the valley's disaster-warning system.

She turned to Mitch, and their eyes met. The only time the siren ever sounded was to alert residents to a life-threatening situation. Both of them were acutely aware that the flood conditions had obviously just been escalated from "potentially dangerous" to "disaster" level.

Total quiet reigned in the center — an unnatural, sudden, and strangely oppressive quiet. Slowly, almost as if on signal, everyone began to move toward the large, wide windows at the front of the building in an attempt to look outside. It was an orderly procession. *Too* orderly, Freddi thought, her own tension swelling at the sight of so many numb expressions and wooden movements.

It was too dark to see anything, and after a few hushed moments, people began to disperse, a few at a time, wandering aimlessly back to the lobby or the cafeteria.

"Still want that coffee?" Mitch asked, taking her arm.

"Desperately — but I think I'll try to find some milk instead." The truth was, Freddi was beginning to feel ill. She'd had no dinner before her harrowing experience at the farm — had, in fact, put nothing except decaffeinated coffee into her stomach since lunch.

"I hope Abby gets here before long," she said as they started toward the open doors of the cafeteria. "I could do with some food."

"They probably have some sandwiches made up by now." Mitch looked at her. "That's right, you didn't have any dinner, did —"

He stopped at the sound of his name. From the information center at the end of the lobby, Tom Robbins was holding a cordless phone to his ear with one hand while gesturing for Mitch with the other.

Tossing his raincoat over a box that had been pushed to one side, Mitch started across the room. Freddi followed.

The policeman clicked off the phone just as they reached him. His eyes went to Freddi, lingering on her face for an instant before he turned to Mitch. "It's the dam," he said, his voice low and tight. "The commissioners say it may not hold."

How strange it was, Freddi thought dimly, to finally hear those words, words she had grown up dreading yet half anticipating over the years. Now that somebody had finally voiced them, they sounded unreal, impossible to grasp.

She looked at Mitch, saw one shoulder lift and fall in a tense jerk. "Who called?"

"Coates. He and one of the county engineers are up at the dam now. He said they've got all the spillways and guards open, but there's debris piling up too fast to clear — it's clogging the main screens and gratings."

"What about an alternate spillway?" asked Mitch tersely.

"Apparently they've already cut one through. Coates said they have men digging a second one a few feet away from the breast of the dam and one more at the west end."

Mitch waited, saying nothing.

"They don't think it will help," Robbins added.

Freddi turned from Mitch to the police officer. "Isn't there anything else they can try?"

Robbins seemed to struggle with his reply. "There *is* one thing. They want to cut through one end of the dam and let part of the water out. It'll divert some of the pressure, and if the dam *does* break, at least the water will go out slower than if it breaks through the middle all at once."

"They're that sure it won't hold?" Mitch's voice was steady, but his face was ashen.

"That's what it sounds like to me. At this point, I think they're looking for a way to save the town." He stopped, glanced down, then raised his eyes to Freddi's. "It would mean that your farm would be completely wiped out, Miss Leigh. They said I should tell you."

For a moment his words seemed to hang between them. Certain she must have misunderstood, Freddi stared at him. "Wiped out?"

Robbins gave a short nod, then looked away. "Your place and the entire bottoms land will take the worst of it." He turned back. "I'm sorry," he added quietly.

Overcome by a sudden wave of dizziness, Freddi was vaguely aware that Mitch had moved closer to her side. "Does she have anything to say about this?" he asked sharply.

"I'm afraid not," replied Robbins. "There are other farms involved, too, but the decision has to be made by the county officials."

"It sounds to me as if it's already been made," Mitch snapped.

"Don't, Mitch," Freddi said quickly. "He's right. They have to do whatever will save the town." She looked at him. "And the campus. You know what it will mean if the dam blows all at once. It'll wipe out everything in the valley." Swallowing thickly against the painful lump in her throat, she again faced Robbins. "When?"

"They're starting right away. They hope to cut through within the next hour."

An hour . . . within one hour the only real home she had ever known — her yesterdays, her history, her roots — would all be lost to her. . . .

"Her car's still out there," Mitch's voice broke into her thoughts.

"It doesn't matter," Freddi said, meaning it. What difference did a car make when her entire past was about to be washed away?

"A Mercedes doesn't matter?" The look Mitch turned on her was both skeptical and incredulous.

"Maybe I could get somebody to drive it in for you, Miss Leigh," Robbins offered.

"The tires are all flat," she told him. "Besides, it's insured and no one has time to bother with that now. There *are* some things, though, that I —" She stopped and turned to Mitch. "I had several photograph albums and some other keepsakes stacked up, ready to store upstairs. Maybe I could still save them if you'd take me — or if you'd let me use your truck."

Mitch turned a questioning glance on Robbins.

The policeman hesitated. "It takes a good fifteen minutes just to drive out there."

Freddi touched Mitch's arm with appeal. "That would still give us at least half an hour. It won't take that long. I have everything ready; all we'd have to do is carry it outside."

His eyes went over her face. "All right. But we go *now*. Right now. You get your things out of my office while I call Abby. If they haven't already left her place, I'm going to tell them to stay put. They'll be better off up there, especially with us gone."

Freddi nodded and began to look around for someone to continue the evacuee list she'd begun.

"Is she alone?" Robbins asked abruptly.

"Abby? No, the Kaines are with her," Mitch answered. "Why?"

"You might want to check on the power

situation up there. It's out in several places across town. I've got a couple of fellows from the faculty checking the auxiliary generators downstairs, so we can at least keep minimal power here. And, Professor —" The policeman's good-natured expression hardened. "You and Miss Leigh need to get going. Don't cut yourselves too close, all right?"

Mitch nodded grimly. "Give that clipboard to one of the Red Cross workers," he told Freddi as he headed toward the phone, "and let's get out of here."

Other than an occasional comment from Mitch about the water that was already creeping across the road in some of the lower places, they were silent during the first few minutes of the ride out to the farm. Freddi limited her responses to a nod or a muttered sound of acknowledgment. The slow-burning fire that had ignited in her stomach earlier was now flaring in earnest. She had all she could do to keep from moaning aloud.

She cast around for something — anything — to take her mind off the pain. "Abby *did* promise to stay at the cabin until we get back, didn't she?"

Mitch nodded, whipping the steering

wheel sharply right to avoid a large clump of mud near the middle of the road. "I talked with Dan, too. They're going back down to my place to stay there until they hear from us. That way, if the power goes out, they can use my generator and still have light. Just to be safe, I asked Tom Robbins to give them a call at my place in half an hour or so." He glanced over at her. "You realize, don't you, that Abby will be glad to have you stay with her as long as you want?"

Freddi managed a smile. "Abby's going to want her living room back eventually. I can stay at the Lodge until I find something, I suppose."

"Freddi?"

She looked at him.

"I'm sorry about the farm," he said quietly. "I wasn't sure it would . . . matter that much to you. But I can see it does."

She turned her face away, unable to deal with the kindness she had seen in his searching gaze. Longing for the privacy to weep, she instead tried to square her shoulders and inject a note of firmness into her voice. "I suppose I didn't realize myself how much it mattered until now," she answered honestly. "It does hurt . . . a lot. But I'll be all right."

"You'll always be all right, won't you, Freddi?" It was more statement than question.

She looked at him, trying to weigh his words, but weakness gripped her, making his features appear hazy for an instant. She had been lightheaded ever since leaving the campus, fighting against the pain radiating hotly from her stomach. She wiped a hand over her eyes and fought for a deep breath. "You could never accept that, could you, Mitch?"

He frowned, not understanding.

"You always did resent my — independence — isn't that what you called it? Why, Mitch?"

He studied her for a moment, slowing for the turnoff to the farm. "Maybe I was afraid," he said quietly.

She shot him a surprised look. Until now, he had always denied the possessiveness responsible for so much conflict between them. "Afraid of *what?*"

"Did it ever occur to you that what you thought was resentment was actually desperation?" He kept his eyes straight ahead as he started down the muddy, deeply furrowed road. "Maybe I thought the only way I could keep you with me . . . was to make you *need* me."

218

His unexpectedly candid answer pierced Freddi's heart.

"All I ever wanted was to be as important to you as you were to me." He suddenly looked very tired — tired and defeated. "But you didn't need me. You didn't need *anyone*. You never did."

Freddi couldn't deny the truth of his accusation. There *had* been a time when she had imagined herself to be just that self-sufficient. Why should Mitch believe she had changed?

Neither of them spoke again until he parked in front of the house. Cutting the engine, he turned to her. "Tell me something, Freddi," he said quietly. "If I hadn't been so paranoid about losing you — if I hadn't tried so desperately to keep you here — would you still have gone away? Did I *drive* you away?"

"*No!*" She leaned across the seat toward him. It was incomprehensible to her that he would blame himself. "No," she emphasized again, sinking weakly back against the seat. "It wasn't you. It was the *writing*."

A world of bitterness filled his eyes. He nodded. "It was *always* the writing, wasn't it, Freddi? Nothing else was ever quite as important to you. You put it first, before everything. Including me."

"Yes," Freddi admitted quietly. "That's exactly what I did. And that's what *you* did with *me*." She squeezed her eyes tightly shut, then opened them. "Oh, Mitch, don't you see? We both made the same mistake. I wrapped all my hopes and dreams and faith in one thing — my writing. But it wasn't big enough. It collapsed under the weight. It failed me. But you did the same thing, Mitch. You made *me* your world. You built your life around me. But I wasn't big enough either, Mitch. So I failed you."

As he sat there, unmoving and silent, Freddi thought she could sense his anger fading to confusion.

"What I had to face," she said urgently, "is that there isn't anyone or anything that won't eventually fail us, that ultimately nothing is . . . enough. Nothing except God." Her voice caught, but she went on. "That's one reason I came back, Mitch. I knew I couldn't really start over again until I faced my past and myself — what I used to be. And until I faced you . . . as I am now."

His head came up. Freddi moved to touch his arm, but something in his eyes stopped her.

She wanted him to reach for her, to hold her. She wanted him to press her head against his shoulder and make the world right again, the way he had always been able to do when they were younger.

Instead, he pulled away from her. "We don't have time for this," he said, his voice strained as he opened the door of the truck.

Wounded by his rejection, Freddi knew a sense of despair like nothing she'd ever felt before. She had to press her hands against the seat of the truck to keep from flinging herself at him and pleading with him to love her again. She ached to tell him now what he had wanted to hear years ago, that she needed him, needed him just as much as he had ever needed her . . . perhaps even more.

The problem was that Mitch no longer cared.

SEVENTEEN

Catchside crouched among the trees, watching Donovan and the dishy writer leave the cabin a little before three. He shook with rage, and his fury, combined with the wet, clammy weather, only made his rash worse. Savagely he raked his fingernails over his arms. It was time to finish this job once and for all.

He had been all set to act before daylight. He even had the gasoline can stashed beneath a decaying tree stump. Within minutes, he would have been inside the cabin. He had to question the old lady, but he didn't plan to waste much time.

It couldn't have been any neater. The five of them together like that — he would have had the job done and been out of town before dawn. Now he'd have to chase them down again.

What would run them out in such a hurry at three o'clock in the morning?

He huddled under the hood of his poncho. A few more minutes — that was all. He'd make his move, and —

He jumped when the front door opened

again. The old woman came out, followed by the blind man and the guide dog, then the blind man's wife.

What was going on?

Catchside inched around the tree, watching as they all piled into the Cherokee and took off up the road, in the direction of the old lady's cabin.

His rage now white-hot, he growled an oath and turned, lumbering back through the woods to retrieve the gas can. He took the hillside with fast, broad steps until he came to the van, hidden behind a dense fringe of pine trees near Donovan's cabin.

Opening the door on the driver's side, he reached across the seat, set the gasoline on the floor, and jumped in behind the wheel.

No more messing around. No more delays. No more killing time in this stinking wet mudhole. If he had to off them one at a time, he'd do it — but whatever he had to do, he was going to do it *now.*

He rammed the key into the ignition and, as soon as the engine caught, roared out of the clearing and onto the road.

EIGHTEEN

Abby's cabin was quiet, unnervingly quiet. The rain had stopped, and Jennifer found the silence almost eerie. There was no pounding on the roof, no rattling of windowpanes, no sheets of water crashing against the siding.

It should have been a relief, but instead, the stillness had put her on edge.

The three of them were at the front door, about to lock up and leave, when darkness suddenly fell over the cabin.

Abby uttered a surprised gasp, and Jennifer groaned aloud, instinctively clutching Daniel's arm. "There goes the power."

Daniel and Sunny stopped, waiting.

"Abby, do you have a flashlight handy?" Jennifer asked, straining to focus her eyes, unable to see anything except shadows. "We may need it to get to the car."

"A flashlight? Yes . . . yes, there's one in my bedroom and another in the kitchen, I think. I'll find one, dear. You stay right here with Daniel."

"Be careful that you don't trip over

224

something," Jennifer cautioned as the older woman started toward the hallway. Still gripping Daniel's arm, she turned back to him. "I'm glad Mitch warned us this might happen."

"He's right; we'll be better off at his place. I hope I can get the generator going. He told me what to do, but you and Abby may have to help."

Jennifer shifted from one foot to the other. "I hope Mitch and Freddi get back soon."

He didn't answer.

"Daniel?"

"They don't have much choice," he finally answered. "A hole's being cut through the dam to relieve some of the pressure on it. In another hour or so, Freddi's farm will be under several feet of water."

"Oh, *Daniel* — no!" Jennifer moved a little closer to him. "Is that why they're going out there? Are they going to try to get her car out?"

"No," Daniel said quietly after a moment. "Mitch said Freddi wanted to get some things out of the house — her grandmother's Bible, photograph albums — souvenirs, mostly."

Somehow Jennifer wasn't surprised that

Freddi was more concerned about family keepsakes than a luxury car. This was the woman she had come to know and respect this week — a woman who had her priorities in order.

Daniel's hand covered hers. "They'll be all right. Mitch isn't about to take any chances, not with —"

He broke off when Sunny barked. "It's all right, girl," Jennifer reassured her. Abby walked up behind them in the hall, and Jennifer took the flashlight from her and aimed its beam at the door.

The retriever barked again, straining impatiently at her harness.

"Sunny, what is *wrong* with you?" Jennifer muttered, glancing at the retriever. "I think she has to go, Daniel," she said, opening the door. "Maybe you'd better take her harness off before we —"

She froze. The flashlight shook in her hand, its wavering light illuminating a huge, black-clad man as he mounted the steps of the cabin. He was wearing a black cap and some sort of goggles.

He had a gun leveled directly at them.

Jennifer screamed, and, behind her, Abby cried out. Sunny went rigid, then flew into a rage, barking and roaring like a wild thing.

It was impossible to tell what happened next, whether Daniel loosened his grip on Sunny's harness in the confusion of the moment, or whether the retriever tore herself free. With one powerful lunge she leaped at the man with the gun, hitting him hard, sinking her teeth into his shoulder.

The man reeled, shouted, and fired the gun into the air. The bullet went wild, and Sunny went crazy.

But he was too big and strong for the small-boned retriever. With the gun still in his hand, he ripped the dog away from his body, hammering one large fist at her head. With a shout of rage, he hurled the retriever out into the yard, where she fell with a thud into the wet grass. She squealed when she hit, then whimpered and lay still.

Daniel shot forward at the sound, but Jennifer threw herself in front of him. *"No, Daniel! Stay back!"* She tried to slam the door, but the man's leg shot forward, forcing the door open with one massive, boot-clad foot.

"Inside," he snapped, shoving all of them back as he moved through the door.

Ashen-faced, Daniel stumbled as the man gave him another hard shove. "I've got to get my dog —"

"I said *move,* jerk! The dog's dead!" Reaching across Daniel, the man yanked the flashlight out of Jennifer's hand.

The gun never wavered as he kicked the door shut behind him. Backing all of them into the living room, he trained the flashlight on Abby. His mouth spread into a cold smile, and Jennifer thought she was going to be sick. In the backwash from the flashlight, his goggle-masked face looked almost demonic.

Evil. It was strong enough that Jennifer took a step backward.

The man tossed a pack of matches from his shirt pocket to Jennifer, aiming the flashlight at an oil lamp on the table. "Light it."

Jennifer's hands shook so violently that she used three matches before she got the wick to catch. When she returned to Daniel and Abby, the older woman looked gray and ill, as if she might lose consciousness at any moment.

"Sit down," the giant growled, waving the gun toward the couch. Jennifer reached for Abby's arm but found her rigid and resistant.

"I said sit *down!*" he roared again, tossing the flashlight across the room.

Jennifer pushed Abby gently onto the couch, then sat down beside her.

Daniel started to follow them, but the man shoved him roughly into a chair by the window. Choking back a cry of dismay, Jennifer half rose to go to him. The man whirled around, turning the gun on her, and she sank back onto the couch.

Daniel's face was a mask of anger, but he merely gripped the arms of the chair, saying nothing.

The man flung his cap onto a nearby table, then reached to pull the goggles up on his forehead.

Abby gasped, and Jennifer clutched her arm, cringing at the small, pale eyes staring at her. Red-rimmed and moist, they looked . . . diseased. Diseased and empty.

He seemed to fill the room with his enormous, intimidating frame. Daniel was a big man, tall and thickly muscled, but Jennifer could see that this . . . lunatic . . . would top Daniel by several inches and probably outweighed him by almost a hundred pounds. He was *immense*.

The man turned his gaze on Abby and stared at her for a long, tense moment. "Remember me, Abigail?" he asked in a deceptively soft voice.

For the first time, Jennifer saw Abby

look directly at him. Abby's wide, frightened eyes fastened on the man's face in a silent look of horror.

He let out a jarring laugh. "Well, now, you couldn't be expected to remember, could you? I don't exist. I'm just some figment of your imagination. A phantom you invented to take the heat off yourself — isn't that what the newspapers said?"

The macabre rictus of a smile widened as he lowered the gun slightly. "Well, guess what, Abigail: you weren't dreaming after all."

NINETEEN

After they had loaded Freddi's things into the truck, Mitch left her alone for a few minutes. All the way out to the farm, he had sensed that she was grieving. She had some good-byes to say, and he felt she would want to be alone to say them.

But it was past time for them to be leaving, and he was getting edgy. He was worried about leaving Abby with Dan and Jennifer, in spite of the fact that he had asked Tom Robbins to check on them. The police had their hands full already; there would be precious little time for anything other than what was happening in town. What if that maniac came looking for Abby? Dan was amazing, but he *was* blind.

Closing the tailgate of the pickup, he looked at his watch, then glanced toward the house. He couldn't give her much longer.

Dawn was finally beginning to fight its way over the ridge, a reluctant daybreak struggling past the heavy, leaden skies. He leaned against the side of the truck for a moment, staring out over the vast, deeply shadowed farmland.

He had a few of his own good-byes to say to this place, he realized. Before he was old enough to hire on at the Lodge, he had worked part-time for Freddi's grandfather. This farm was almost as familiar to him as his own place on the mountain. And the memories it held for him were even dearer.

He almost felt that if he looked long enough he would see Freddi racing across the field, her hair tucked under the ever-present baseball cap as she dared him to try to catch her. Or maybe he'd catch a glimpse of her perched on the tire swing in the old maple down by the dairy barn, urging him to push her higher. Or sitting on the top step of the front porch on a Saturday night, waiting for him to pull up in his truck and take her to town.

He closed his eyes in an effort to shut out the memories, unwillingly replacing them with the words she had spoken on the way out here — words she had seemed so desperate for him to understand. Somehow the truth of what she had said to him repeated itself over and over again in his spirit. . . .

"*. . . I wrapped all my hopes and dreams and faith in one thing. . . . But it wasn't big* *enough. . . . It failed me. But you did the same thing, Mitch. You made me your world, you built your life around me. But I wasn't big enough either. . . . So I failed you. What I had to face is that there isn't anyone or anything that won't eventually fail us, that ultimately nothing is . . . enough . . . except God. . . ."*

Mitch opened his eyes. How was it, he wondered, that she had been able to accept something he had known but had managed to suppress for so long?

For years he had blamed her. Then, for a time, he had hated her — or tried to. Finally, he had enshrined her, turning her into a monument, something only his memories could contain. But always there had been that unspoken, uncomfortable awareness that he had somehow distorted the order of things, that he had made her *too* important, had placed her where no human being had a right to stand — between him and his God.

Freddi had accused him of making her his world, of building his life around her.

And he had. To the exclusion of almost everything else. He had loved her too much, always too much. More than life, maybe even more than his God.

How could she have lived up to such an

obsessive love? How could *anyone?*

Freddi had been through . . . something, that much was evident. And whatever it was, it had brought her face-to-face with her own crisis of faith: the weaknesses, the stumbling blocks, and, yes, the *pride* that had been part of her nature for years.

But what about *him?* Hadn't Freddi been *his* stumbling block . . . his "weakness" all this time? He had spent years blaming her for not being bigger than life —

When all the time I should have realized that nothing . . . and no one . . . is bigger than life except you, Lord.

It seemed that Freddi had learned the truth long before he had. Suddenly, he desperately needed to talk with her, to hear for himself whatever it was that had brought her to this place — back to the Ridge, yes, but more important, brought her to a new walk of faith.

With a stab of frustration, he realized that the answers to his questions would have to wait until later. The first thing he had to do was to get both of them safely back to campus.

When he didn't find her inside, he thought he knew where to look. He went around to the back of the house, and, sure enough, she was down at the gazebo.

The small, white latticework building — another indulgence of her grandfather's — stood atop a gentle swell of ground facing the ridge. It had been her playhouse, then her "dreamhouse," as she'd called it. She had gone there to write her stories on summer afternoons. Later the two of them had gone there to talk and plan their future together.

Mitch wondered if she remembered the first time he had told her he loved her. It had been inside that gazebo in the middle of a spring rainstorm.

As he got closer, he saw that she was leaning forward, both hands pressed palms down on the narrow, scrolled banister. Her back was to him, and for a moment he thought she was ill. His heart lurched, but then he heard her and realized she was praying. He couldn't be sure, but he thought she was also weeping.

He hesitated, wondering if he should walk away and leave her alone. Then he took another step toward the gazebo, listening, despite his reluctance to intrude on what was obviously a very private moment.

"I know I told you I'd give it all up, if that's what it takes. And I will, Lord — the writing, the career, the farm — everything. . . ."

Mitch's heart started to break. She was

hunched over even more now, her thin shoulders — too thin, he noted — heaving slightly with her words.

"... *But you understand, don't you, that right now I feel as if I'm being torn to pieces? It isn't the farm, Lord, although losing it will be like losing a piece of my heart. But I'll get over that in time, and I know you'll help me put my life back together again eventually. I know you will...."*

Mitch choked back tears, as if her words were being ripped from his own throat.

"... *But I don't think the pain of losing Mitch will ever be over, Lord ... not really. I didn't know it would hurt this much; I didn't think anything could hurt this much...."* She faltered, then went on. *"Oh, Lord, he was your gift to me ... and I think you meant me to be your gift to him, but we got things all mixed up and ended up putting the gift before the Giver."*

Mitch squeezed his eyes shut, letting the import of her words roll over him. Wearily, he rubbed his hands down his face, thinking for a moment that the moisture on his fingertips was rain. Only when he opened his eyes did he realize that the wetness spilling down his cheeks was from his own tears.

He moved now, closing the distance between them, stepping up into the gazebo and putting a hand on her shoulder.

For a moment he didn't think she was even aware of his presence. But, finally, she straightened and turned to face him. Mitch's gaze traced the tears down her cheeks; then he touched his fingers to them as he searched beyond the pain in her eyes for something else, something he had ached to see throughout all the years between them.

"I'm sorry, Freddi-Leigh," he said softly, remembering another lifetime of moments like this, when he had teased her or hurt her feelings in some foolish, unintentional way. "I didn't mean to make you cry."

Her eyes lifted to his, questioning, seeking.

Mitch trapped her hand in his and tugged at it, drawing her closer. His other hand went to her damp hair, then to her cheek. "When there's time, I want you to tell me the rest of your story."

Her look was puzzled, but when she would have questioned him, he pressed a finger to her lips, stopping her. "I want to be sure I understand what you were trying to tell me on the way out here. All of it. But not now. There's no time. I'm going to ask you just one question, and then we have to leave. All right?"

She nodded, tilting her head even more as she waited.

Calling forth another memory, Mitch took both of her hands in his. "Will you be my girl, Freddi-Leigh?" he whispered. "For always?"

Freddi went deathly still, searching his eyes. Mitch was aware of her trembling as his hands went to her shoulders. "Will you, Freddi-Leigh?" He kissed her gently at the corner of her mouth. *It was yesterday again. . . .*

With a small cry, she came into his arms. Mitch kissed her once more, returning his heart to her, asking once more for the gift of her love.

He looked at her, saw her smiling at him through lingering tears. "Say it," he urged, gently stroking her hair, pushing it back from her temples.

"I'll always be your girl, Mitch Donovan. For as long as the river runs, I'll be your girl."

She remembered. . . .

When he kissed her this time, he was promising her what she had just promised him. *Forever . . .*

Daybreak rose in his heart at the same time it came up over the mountain.

★ ★ ★

"I wish we had left sooner," he said worriedly as the pickup bumped onto the dirt road leading away from the farm. "We're cutting it too close."

He went on, talking mostly to himself, trying to give vent to the swell of anxiety that was about to choke him. Freddi was sitting close to him, as she had years before when they were teenagers. He put his arm around her shoulders and pulled her a little closer. He felt better. Just having her back in his life made everything better.

"First thing when we get back to town, we'll get a Civil Defense boat and go up to my place. I want to get Abby and the others out of there, down to the campus where they're not so isolated."

"You think we'll need a boat this soon?"

He veered sharply left to avoid a deep pit in the road. "Probably not," he answered distractedly, straightening the steering wheel. "But I don't want to chance getting stuck on the other side of the glen."

"You're not worried about the campus?"

He shook his head. "Even if the dam blows, the extra spillway will slow the water down enough to save the campus. It won't have the momentum to climb that high. It's the town and the bottoms that will take the worst." He paused, then added, "I just hope we did the right thing, leaving them at my place."

When Freddi didn't answer, he looked at her. Her face was sickly white, her mouth contorted with pain. She was hugging her midsection as if she feared she might break in two.

"Freddi? What's wrong?"

She shook her head, saying nothing. Moving away from him, she reached for her purse and fumbled inside it until she pulled out a small white bottle.

"What's that? Are you sick?"

"I'm all right," she grated between clenched teeth.

He watched her open the bottle and take three deep swallows before replacing the cap. "What is that stuff? What's it for?"

"It's just . . . Mylanta," she admitted grudgingly. "I have an ulcer."

Keeping his eyes on the road, he frowned. "An ulcer? Is that serious?"

She uttered a choking laugh. "Mitch, you are probably the only person in my entire world who doesn't know all about ulcers."

"I know about ulcers," he said, with a trace of defensiveness. "I just don't know how serious they are."

"Mine . . . was better. As long as I avoid junk-food binges and stress, I can live with it. I guess I haven't done so well with either this week."

No sooner were the words out of her mouth than she jerked against the seat, moaning softly.

Freeing one hand, Mitch touched her forehead. Her skin was cold, yet clammy with perspiration. "Can I do anything?"

She shook her head weakly.

"Is it always this painful?"

"No. Not always," she said, gritting her teeth.

Watching the road, he skimmed a kiss over the top of her head. "You just need some good old-fashioned country living," he said. "That'll take care of the stress."

"Right. This week has done a lot to eliminate the stress in my life."

"Well, you'll see. We'll get some weight on you and —"

He broke off, interrupted by several loud booms — like thunder or a series of explosions.

His eyes went to the rearview mirror and locked on the sight of an enormous wall of water bearing down on the valley.

It took a few seconds for reality to pierce his panic. "Here it comes," he choked out, yanking his arm free to grip the wheel with both hands. "Get over there and buckle up — now!"

At first it looked like a dark, dense layer of fog rolling in over the valley, treetop high. Mitch rolled down his window a little so he could hear, only to be jolted by the thundering noise.

White-faced, Freddi slid toward the door and snapped on her seat belt, then whipped around. He heard her gasp, felt her clutch his shoulder. "Mitch . . ."

"I know . . . I know . . . just hang on."

He slammed the accelerator to the floor, his eyes on the rearview mirror. Behind them, churning waves of water several stories high pushed shapeless masses of debris in front of them, flinging trees and chunks of earth as if they were nothing.

When they reached the intersection of the main highway, Mitch's eyes made a frenzied sweep in all directions; then he shot left onto the road.

He tilted the rearview mirror a fraction. The wall was closing in on them. It had to be moving twenty miles an hour or more, sucking up everything in its path, grinding it up, tossing it out, gaining momentum with every second.

"Are we going to make it?" Freddi's

voice was oddly quiet, even steady. She had never been the hysterical type, but Mitch wouldn't have blamed her if she had opened her mouth and started to scream. He wasn't all that far from it himself.

"We'll make it," he said tightly. He wished he felt even half as confident as he tried to sound.

Her hand still clung to his shoulder as she again turned to look behind them. He heard her catch a sharp breath.

"We'll be all right," he reassured her. "We're going to make it." He could feel her fear and was nearly choking on his own.

In another quarter mile they would reach the bridge over Job's Trace, the lowest point of the bottoms where the valley began to narrow, then merge and climb upward until it became one with the ridge. If they got that far, he could outrun the rolling monster behind him.

It was coming down on them fast now, unleashing total destruction on everything in its path. He stabbed again at the accelerator, but it was already to the floor.

They were on the downhill run.

Then he saw the bridge — or what had been the bridge before the swollen stream had pushed it up into the air. Pieces of steel and concrete littered both sides of the road, and part of a narrow pillar stood up-ended in the roiling water. Nothing else.

Mitch sucked in an enormous gulp of air, gripping the wheel until pain shot through his knuckles.

Beside him, Freddi reared back hard against the seat, her knuckles pressed against her mouth.

Mitch grabbed one last look in the rear-view mirror and knew he had to go for it.

"Hang on!"

With one mighty rebel yell, he hunched forward over the wheel. The Ranger lifted off, bouncing them up off the seat, throwing them hard against their seat belts as it leaped across the stream and landed front end first on the other side. The bumper scraped asphalt for a good ten feet until the lighter back end of the pickup finally touched down.

He took the hill full tilt, swallowing down the taste of raw panic that threatened to choke him. Fishtailing up the mud-washed hill, Mitch shot a frantic glance at the rear-view mirror. The wall of water, like a monster whose rampage had been temporarily thwarted, had crested only feet below them and was now surging madly over the fields, gathering new power as it continued on its death route toward the valley.

Mitch's heart pounded painfully against his chest. But he couldn't ease up now. The town was only seconds away from destruction. He had to get to the campus.

But Freddi was with him, and they were safe. He couldn't let himself think of anything beyond this moment.

"Didn't I tell you we'd make it?" he said in a woefully unsteady voice.

When she didn't answer, he looked over to see her draining the upended Mylanta bottle in one continuous gulp.

TWENTY

Abby's face was blank, her eyes dull. Catchside had been grilling her for nearly an hour, hammering away at her with relentless cruelty that made Jennifer want to scream at him in rage.

Despite his tenacity, Abby had told him nothing. In fact, so convincing was her blank bewilderment that Jennifer could almost believe she had somehow been drawn back into the depths of the amnesia. More likely, though, Abby's attempts to mislead her interrogator were motivated by a desire to protect everyone else.

Jennifer no longer believed it would make the slightest difference. With dreadful certainty, she felt they were all doomed, no matter what they did or didn't know about Abby's past.

By dawn, the intimidating giant was growing noticeably frustrated and impatient. As he stood in the middle of the living room, he seemed to fill every inch of open space with a scarcely contained, malevolent energy. If possible, he was even more menacing in the gray light of morning than he had been in the shadowed glow of the oil lamp. The man was obviously deranged, a volatile psychotic whose actions were hopelessly unpredictable. One minute he would be soft-voiced and unnervingly calm, the next, crude and almost savagely irrational.

Abby's composure under fire astonished Jennifer. Other than the repeated pulling of her hands in her lap and the cast of horror in her eyes, she seemed isolated, almost invulnerable to her tormentor's verbal abuse.

"All right, Abigail, if that's the best you've got for me, we might just as well get this over with." He was back to his quiet-voiced calm, which somehow frightened Jennifer even more than his raving.

"It's a real shame about your . . . *amnesia,* Abigail. I was kind of hoping to find out why old Taylor hates your hide the way he does."

When Abby gave him a blank look, he went on, goading her with a mocking smile. "I never did believe it was just the money, not that he isn't a hungry old bird. It occurs to me that maybe it was you who tipped his brother off about the scam Taylor was running on the side."

He watched Abby as if to measure her reaction.

When there was none, he continued to ramble, his tone deceptively low, his words quick and detached. "Yeah, when that righteous hubby of yours found out about old Taylor using some of his fancy resorts to front a drug operation, that's when he started making noises about changing his will, right?"

With what appeared to be genuine confusion, Abby merely stared at him.

He glanced at Jennifer, then Daniel. "Say, that's right. If Abigail here is telling the truth about not knowing who she is or anything about her past, that means you don't know either, right?" He grinned. "Well, let me introduce you. This is Abigail Chase, one very wealthy widow. Old Abigail here, she did all right for herself. Went from running her own dinky little catering business to managing the entire food operation for Chase resorts. And then topped it off by marrying the boss."

He fixed a hard glare on Abby. "I think you must be a lot smarter than you look, Abigail. You couldn't lose, could you? And old Taylor, he couldn't win. First, you cheat him out of a big chunk of his inheritance by marrying his brother, then Roger decides to cut him out of the will altogether. Nice and neat."

"And that's where you came in, isn't it?" Daniel said from his chair by the window. "You were supposed to make sure the will never got changed — and get rid of Abby and Chase's granddaughter in the process."

Catchside turned to him. "Ding-ding, blind man, you figured it out. And if you got that much, you probably know why I'm here." He looked at Daniel with a trace of scornful amusement.

"So Taylor Chase can collect on the will. Which he can't, until Abby's . . . death . . . is legally established," Daniel said grimly. "But just how do you intend to go about proving she's dead without implicating yourself?"

The contempt in Catchside's expression deepened. "Simple. The rest of you get this —" He hefted the gun. "And a trip down the river. But Abigail, she gets special treatment — a quick, clean drowning. Later, someone will find her washed up on the riverbank, with proper identification — which I just happen to have with me." He sneered, tapping the pocket of his black shirt. "And I'll go back to being the man who never was."

Suddenly his mood did an abrupt shift. "I thought you said the other two would be back soon," he growled at Jennifer.

When she nodded grudgingly, he stared at her for another few seconds. "Get up," he snarled. "Maybe by the time I'm done with the three of you, they'll be here."

Jennifer didn't move. Her gaze went from his face to the gun.

"I said *move!* Now! We're all going for a little walk down by the riverside."

Clutching Abby's hand, Jennifer helped her up from the couch. Her own hands were shaking violently, but she made herself face Catchside. "What are you going to do to us?"

"You want to know what I'm going to do?" He gave her a contemptuous smirk. "See this gun?" He pointed it directly at her head. "Bang-bang."

Jennifer jumped back, her heart thundering as he leveled the gun at Daniel and silently mouthed the word again.

"Then you'll just get . . . washed away. Fish food. And when Donovan and the writer show up, they'll join you. Well, Donovan, anyway." He paused and gave a leering smile. "I may want to talk to the lady writer a while first."

"No!" The sudden wail of protest came from Abby.

Catchside looked at her. "Sorry, Abigail,

but that's how it is. Come on, now, let's get moving. I'm sick of this mudhole town. The sooner I can split, the better."

"Just how do you expect to get out?" The quiet, deliberate question came from Daniel, who had risen from his chair and was standing near the window.

Catchside whipped around, staring at him. "What do you mean, how do I expect to get out?" he mimicked nastily. "The same way I came in, jerk."

Daniel shook his head. "Wrong. There *is* no way out." His voice was unnaturally soft as he went on. "All the roads are closed by now. Most of the town is under water. And the dam's expected to collapse any minute. You're trapped. Just like the rest of us."

Jennifer stared at her husband in confusion. He sounded . . . peculiar. He was almost smiling — a baiting, scornful smile that wasn't at all like Daniel.

Catchside's eyes darted to the window. Licking his lips nervously, he snapped, "Shut up, blind man."

"It's true. You're not going anywhere."

Enraged, Catchside took a step toward Daniel. "*I'm* going anywhere I want to, jerk! *You're* the one who's going down the river."

Daniel uttered a short, explosive laugh

of contempt. With a roar of fury, Catchside lunged for him.

"Jennifer — get out! You and Abby, get out of here!"

Suddenly the reason for Daniel's odd behavior crystallized in Jennifer's mind. This was what he wanted, to goad Catchside into jumping him so she and Abby would have a chance to get away.

She felt Abby sway, then break free. Before Jennifer could stop her, Abby threw herself at Catchside, grappling for the gun. The madman turned, and Daniel pitched forward, slamming against the giant's back.

Catchside staggered, then planted himself in place, firing the gun in the air.

With an inhuman fury, he attempted to throw Abby off, but she clung to him, clawing at his face as she tried to wrench the gun free.

Jennifer lunged to help just as the gun exploded again.

Abby reeled, then fell. Screaming, Jennifer dropped to her knees, watching in horror as blood spread across Abby's shoulder, soaking the fabric of her dress.

Frantically Jennifer looked around for something to stop the blood. Seeing nothing, she ripped the cloth belt of her slacks free, tore the lace curtain from the window, and tied a piece of it around Abby's shoulder.

She turned around in time to see Catchside throw Daniel off and level the gun at his chest.

"*No!*" With Abby still in her arms, Jennifer screamed a cry of warning. Daniel stopped, and Catchside swung the gun toward Jennifer.

"Try it again, blind man," he said in a menacing growl, "and I'll kill you and your woman right here, right now."

Daniel lifted both hands in the air, palms outward, in a gesture of surrender, then stood without moving.

Catchside trained the gun on Jennifer. "Get up."

"She's hurt, I can't —"

With one step, he moved to yank the semiconscious Abby roughly out of Jennifer's arms as if she were a rag doll. "*I said . . . get . . . up!*"

Unwilling to let him see her cower, Jennifer struggled to control her shivering.

"We're going to the river," Catchside said almost tonelessly. "You take him." He motioned Jennifer toward Daniel with the gun. "The two of you do exactly what I tell you to do, or I'll finish the old lady now."

Jennifer took a step toward Daniel, then another. Touching him with a trembling hand, she felt the muscles of his forearm tense. "Just do what he says," he warned her, his voice hard and angry.

They left the cabin, Jennifer and Daniel in front, with Catchside behind them, dragging Abby lifelessly along at his side.

When they reached the bottom of the steps, Jennifer stopped, choking out a cry of despair. Sunny was still sprawled limply in the wet grass, her eyes closed.

As if he had seen, Daniel again squeezed her hand. "Sunny?" he asked in a whisper.

"Yes. Oh, Daniel . . ." She broke off, unable to finish.

"She's dead, isn't she?" he asked dully.

Jennifer's eyes burned with unshed tears as she turned to Catchside. "Please . . . let me see about the dog."

"The dog's dead! Now move!"

She had never seen the kind of anger that surfaced in Daniel at that instant, an anger she knew was fed as much by grief for his beloved Sunny as by his fury toward Catchside. She felt him press her arm. "Don't give up, Jennifer," he grated under his breath. "We'll get out of this."

"Oh, Daniel . . . there's nothing we can do," she whispered. "He's *huge* —"

"The Lord's bigger. And he's on *our* side."

"*Shut up* — both of you!" Catchside punched Jennifer in the back with the pistol, and she stumbled.

Fear and hopelessness washed over her as the gunman prodded them down the thickly wooded hillside to the riverbank. Once she started to pray that Mitch and Freddi would return in time to help, but her prayer faltered. She no longer believed that even all of them together could stop this insane monster.

At the bottom of the hill, Catchside stopped, motioning them toward an immense ash tree.

Keeping the gun trained on them, he began to drag the now unconscious Abby closer to the edge of the riverbank. The ground sloped down several inches toward the water, but the swollen, turbulent river was spilling across the bank, shooting up and over the small rise of mud-slicked ground as it gathered strength for its descent to the valley.

Hauling Abby to the very edge of the bank, Catchside stooped and grasped her by the waist. He started to drag her into the water with the clear intention of drowning her.

Unexpectedly, she roused and twisted in his arms, throwing him off balance. He stumbled in the mud, shoving Abby toward the water as he slipped.

Jennifer cried out as she saw Abby stagger and reel backward, clutching wildly at Catchside to save herself. The force of her weight pulling at him on the slippery bank was enough to dislodge the giant. He staggered, then pitched forward, dropping the gun as he toppled over and crashed into the water.

"Daniel — they fell in!" Jennifer screamed. "Abby will drown! She's barely conscious!"

Daniel was already moving. Ripping his shirt from his body and tossing his shoes aside, he groped for Jennifer's hand.

"I'm going in — you'll have to guide me from here!"

"No, Daniel, you can't —"

"Just take me to the edge of the bank!"

Jennifer hesitated. When he started to step out on his own, she reluctantly guided him to the water's edge.

He stood listening for a long, tense moment. "Where are they?"

Jennifer looked from Daniel to the river. Already drifting out away from the bank, Abby seemed to be just barely keeping herself afloat. Only a few feet away, Catchside, his face set in a look of shock, bobbed heavily in the water.

Jennifer turned to Daniel. His face was taut, his breathing shallow. He was poised, obviously waiting for her to prompt him.

She glanced down at the cotton slacks she was wearing. Making her decision, she pulled her blouse free from the waistband and kicked off her shoes.

"I'm going in with you." The steadiness of her voice amazed her.

Jennifer wasn't a good swimmer. It was a family joke, her lack of prowess in the water contrasted with the skill of her Olympian husband. But Daniel needed her eyes. And Abby needed Daniel.

"The Lord has a way of putting us exactly where he wants us. . . ."

As Daniel's earlier words echoed from somewhere in a distant recess of her mind, Jennifer suddenly saw the truth. At this moment, she was in the right place at the right time.

In that instant everything around her seemed to freeze and hang suspended, and Jennifer saw herself from an entirely different perspective. Without understanding why, she realized that the Lord was giving her this moment, this brief blink in time to catch a glimpse of herself as he viewed her . . . standing where he wanted her to stand, being what he wanted her to be, doing what he wanted her to do.

Standing in his will . . . standing where he had placed her.

I understand now, Lord, I really do. I don't have to do anything great or newsworthy or world-changing. I don't have to be a celebrity or a headline-getter. I only have to be the person you made me to be and live the life you've given me to live . . . today, right where I am, just as I am.

She took a deep breath and gripped her husband's hand, then stepped out. "Now, Daniel!"

He hesitated only an instant, then sucked in a breath and went off the bank, surging left as soon as he hit the water. Jennifer followed him, determined, in spite of her fear.

"Stay to my right if you can," Daniel told her, pulling easily through the turbulent water. "Does Catchside still have the gun?"

"No — he dropped it when he fell in!" Jennifer had all she could do to stay with him. The water was cold, dangerously cold for a poor swimmer, and the current seemed to be picking up momentum every second. Her legs felt sandbagged, and her arms were already beginning to ache.

"Are you all right?" Daniel was pulling away from her.

"I can't keep up with you!"

He slowed his stroke. "How far away is Abby?"

Jennifer squeezed her eyes shut against the sting of the water, then opened them. "Not far. I can reach her."

She shot a look at Catchside, surprised to see that the behemoth didn't seem to be doing as well in the water as *she* was. He was still several feet away from Abby, swimming haltingly, awkwardly, as if something were pulling him under. Those heavy boots couldn't be helping.

The water was full of wood, stones, and other debris being carried by the current. Jennifer screamed when a large, heavy limb caught Abby on the side of the head. The older woman's arms swept out once, then went limp.

Seeing his chance, Catchside pulled through the water until he reached her.

"*He's got her!* Daniel — I think Abby blacked out!"

"If I can pull him off her, do you think you can get her out of the water?"

"I'll . . . try." Jennifer was gasping for air now. She was already tired, more tired than she wanted Daniel to know. And the raging current was quickly forcing all of them downhill and farther away from the bank.

Out of the corner of her eye, she saw an enormous chunk of wood rolling toward her. She swerved and cut right. It hurtled by, missing her by only inches.

"Glide as much as you can," Daniel warned. "Don't try to fight the current. Just keep moving toward the two of them and let the water carry you. I'll try to get behind him, but you'll have to guide me."

Jennifer's lungs felt seared, and pain shot down the entire length of her body. She couldn't answer him.

They were almost on top of Abby and Catchside now. Catchside tried to turn and pull away, pushing Abby's head under water as he moved.

"*No-o-o!*" Jennifer fought for the strength to reach Abby. "Daniel — to your right! *He's to your right!*"

Turning, Daniel shoved off, circling behind Catchside as smoothly as if he could see.

Like some kind of immense sea monster, Catchside bobbed up, then down, his eyes bugging when Daniel grasped him around the neck from behind.

This was her chance. Jennifer summoned all the strength she had and surged toward Abby.

Daniel had the giant by the throat, kneeing him in the back. Although Catchside had an obvious size advantage, he was clumsy and uncertain in the water. Daniel was clearly in control.

Jennifer grappled for Abby's arms, ducking Catchside's fist as he tried to shove her away with one hand and throw Daniel off with the other.

Wrapping Catchside with both arms, Daniel shouted, "Take her, Jennifer!"

Jennifer wrested Abby free and pulled her into a headlock. "I've got her, Daniel!"

"Get out of here! Hurry!"

Jennifer bobbed uncertainly. "I'm not leaving you —"

"You've *got* to! *Do it,* Jennifer! While you've still got the strength! Don't try to swim against the current — go downriver and float toward the bank!"

Jennifer knew with sick certainty that she had no choice if she didn't want to risk both her life and Abby's. Reluctantly, she began to swim. "I'll come back, Daniel!" she called out as she turned. "Just as soon as I get Abby out of the water, I'll come back!"

"No!" Daniel roared, his face contorted with the effort of trying to keep Catchside subdued. "You'll be too tired! I won't be able to find you in this current! Stay on the bank!"

Still, Jennifer hesitated, watching with fear as Daniel fought to keep Catchside from breaking free. Finally, with one last look at her husband and the madman in his grasp, she began to pull right, letting the current carry her as she struggled to tow the unconscious Abby to safety.

It was like trying to uproot a mountain. A mountain in the sea. For the first time in his life, Daniel felt small. This lunatic was going to kill them both unless he could somehow knock him out.

The guy was enormous — and crazy! Daniel knew an instant of raw panic when the enraged giant pulled them both under water, hurling them against the torrential current of the river.

His own strength was beginning to drain when he finally managed to surface, still clinging to the struggling Catchside. Shooting upward, Daniel crashed down on the giant, riding him as if he were a sea animal, trying to push his head down into the water at the same time.

His own head felt as if it might explode any second. The roaring in his ears swelled to an almost unbearable pitch, and he gasped for air as he tried to keep Catchside's face in the water.

. . . Save me, O God, for the waters have come up to my neck. . . . I have come into the deep waters; the floods engulf me. . . .

The colossus beneath Daniel began to buck in the water, trying to throw him off. Like a crazed bull, Catchside pitched and lunged, but Daniel held on, afraid even to try to throw a punch for fear he'd lose control.

. . . I am worn out calling for help. . . . deliver me from those who hate me, from the deep waters. . . . answer me quickly, for I am in trouble. . . .

He *was* in trouble. His legs were cramping, his arm muscles knotting, his lungs rebelling against the torturous pressure in his chest. He could feel the increasing sweep of current as wood and other debris rushed past them in the water. This end of the river was swelling from the effect of the extra cut-through at the dam. He had all he could do to hang on to the madman beneath him.

Then, dimly, Daniel became aware of a difference in the cacophony of the river.

The roar in his head had changed. It wasn't in his ears at all but seemed to be rising from the water. His head snapped around, and a fresh burst of energy swept him upward.

For an instant he thought he might be about to lose consciousness, that he had only imagined the sound. He shook his head, trying to clear it.

No . . . it was real.

The thunder in his head had become the sound of a powerboat.

"Hang on, Dan! We've got you!" somebody yelled.

Mitch?

He was hearing not one engine but *two*. Both close by.

A different voice yelled out. "*This is the police!* There's a gun on your head, mister. Give it up! You're under arrest!"

Daniel felt somebody grab him under his arms and start to haul him up out of the water and into the boat. He tried to help but couldn't seem to move his arms or legs. Finally, he felt himself pulled aboard, then gently lowered to the floor of the boat.

"Easy, Dan . . . easy . . . we've got you." It *was* Mitch.

A gunshot crashed over the roar of the

river. Closer now, the unfamiliar voice again shouted. "I said, give it up! You don't get more than one warning!"

There was an ominous quiet, about the pause of a heartbeat, then, "They've got him, Dan!"

"Mitch —"

"It's all right." Mitch grasped his arm. "The police have Catchside! It's over."

"The police . . . how . . ."

"When Freddi and I got back into town, Tom Robbins was just getting ready to come up here. He had been trying to call you, and when he couldn't get an answer at my place or Abby's, we grabbed a boat and started up the river. A couple of state policemen followed us."

Daniel heard Mitch catch his breath. "They've got Catchside in the other boat. Everything's OK, Dan."

Daniel tried to push himself up. *"Jennifer —"*

"She's fine. She and Freddi are on the bank with Abby."

"Is Abby . . . ?"

"Abby's all right. She's lost some blood, but she's OK. Thanks to you and Jennifer."

"You're sure Jennifer is all right? She's not very strong in the water —"

"She's *fine,* Dan. Honest. She's exhausted, but she's fine." Mitch stopped, then added, "Jennifer saved Abby's life."

"They made it. . . ." Daniel could feel himself slipping, drifting off. . . .

Then he heard it — a sound as familiar to his ears as his own voice. He forced his mind to focus — there! He *had* heard it.

"Sunny?"

Again came the bark. From a distance that could have been inches or miles, he heard her bark again.

". . . Sunny . . ."

"Sunny's OK, Dan." Mitch's voice was no more than an echo, as if he were calling out from the other end of a long tunnel. "She's going to be fine. She's with Jennifer."

Daniel smiled and started to mumble words of thanks but found his lips were numb.

EPILOGUE

Friday evening

The entire hillside — above and below the campus — was covered with people and flickering lanterns.

From the platform that had been erected for the benefit concert, Jennifer could look out past the crowds thronging the mountain to see the town of Derry Ridge — what was left of it. The flood had left in its wake only mud, debris, and devastation. The additional spillway cut through the dam at the last minute had been enough to save the valley from annihilation, but even those who had been fortunate enough to escape total loss had suffered some degree of damage.

And yet they were here. *Everyone* was here tonight, gathered for a concert designed to give encouragement to the audience while collecting vital funds to help rebuild the town.

Mitch and the festival committee, with Daniel's cooperation, had put together this last-minute concert, turning it into a benefit event for the entire community. Much prayer and hurried planning had gone into the evening — with incredible results.

Jennifer had long stood in awe of Daniel's ability as a musician and a performer, but never before tonight had she seen him capture an entire audience quite so quickly and completely. It seemed as if God had reached down in a special way tonight to empower and bless her husband's music ministry — a ministry that had already reached countless hearts throughout the country.

As she watched, both Daniel and Mitch came back onto the platform for the conclusion of the concert. Along with the other singers and musicians, Jennifer stepped forward, then went to stand beside her husband.

She exchanged smiles with Freddi and Abby, both seated as close as possible to the makeshift stage. Abby's arm was in a sling, but she looked wonderful.

Abby's recently reacquired fortune was apparently going to make little difference in her lifestyle. Just that morning she had revealed her plans to all of them: to remain right where she was, in the cabin she loved, continuing with her work in the campus cafeteria. Her only concession to the Chase legacy was a suggestion to Mitch that she might want to add an extra room or two onto the back of the cabin.

". . . So my grandchildren can spend weekends with me as often as they want," she had explained.

"You have *grandchildren*, Abby?" Mitch had questioned with a startled look.

"Well, not *yet*, dear." Abby's glance had darted to Freddi. "But I should imagine I will *eventually*."

Jennifer let her gaze drift to Freddi, fancifully imagining her in bridal white, since that was most likely what the stunning young author would be wearing when they next met. The wedding would take place early in the fall, Mitch had announced just before the concert. "*Very* early in the fall." He had thrown a challenging look at Freddi, who merely grinned a silent assent.

Jennifer's smile faded for an instant at the fleeting, unpleasant thought of Floyd Catchside. He would never murder anyone else once the courts were finished with him, she thought with grim satisfaction. Not only was he being held for the murders of Roger and Melissa Chase, but law enforcement agencies throughout the country — throughout the *world* — were lining up to question him about numerous other unsolved killings.

The sound of Daniel's voice roused her from her thoughts, and she turned toward him as he spoke.

"I know there are hundreds — *thousands* — of you out there tonight who have lost everything: your homes, your material possessions, all that you've worked for over the years."

Jennifer moved a little closer to him. She could sense the burden on his heart as he hesitated. But when he spoke again, his voice was firm and strong.

"As we were trying to put together this concert, I asked the Lord to give me some word of hope, some message of encouragement for those of you who might need it most. Just this morning, I remembered something Mitch Donovan said to me our first day here, something that many of you may have already heard." He paused, then went on. "It's a truth that once sustained me through a loss of my own — the loss of my sight.

"Tonight, I pray that the Lord will write it on my heart — and yours — so we can draw on it throughout the days ahead, whenever we need to be reminded of our legacy in the Lord."

The mountain was hushed as Daniel's voice rang out strong and clear. "Sometimes," he said, smiling with love at the people he could see only in his heart, "sometimes you have to get to the point where Jesus Christ is all you *have* . . . before you realize that Jesus Christ is all you *need.*"

The words drifted off into the night fog now softly enveloping the mountain. After a moment, Daniel began to sing, softly at first, then with rousing reassurance. Soon the night rang with thousands of voices lifted in faith and hope. . . .

"On Christ, the solid Rock, I stand,
All other ground is sinking sand,
All other ground is sinking sand."

The employees of Thorndike Press hope you have enjoyed this Large Print book. All our Large Print titles are designed for easy reading, and all our books are made to last. Other Thorndike Press Large Print books are available at your library, through selected bookstores, or directly from us.

For information about titles, please call:

(800) 257-5157

To share your comments, please write:

Publisher
Thorndike Press
P.O. Box 159
Thorndike, Maine 04986